THE KISS OF DEATH

It started with a mosquito bite. Millions of people the world over cursed the little pests that came with the arrival of summer—cursed, and slapped the annoyance into a bloody pulp, and went on about their business.

But some people were unable to go on with the normal routine of life. What came as a bite turned quickly into soreness of throat, loss of voice, and then complete paralysis! And soon people all over the world were dying, painfully. Z5 was always interested in events out of the ordinary, and particularly so when it seemed as though the mysterious plague were aimed at the destruction of that organization!

THE PLAGUE OF SILENCE
John Creasey

PRESTIGE BOOKS • NEW YORK

THE PLAGUE OF SILENCE

Copyright © 1948 by John Creasey
All rights reserved
Printed in the U.S.A.

PRESTIGE BOOKS INC. • 18 EAST 41ST STREET
NEW YORK, N.Y. 10017

CONTENTS

Book I
THE FIRST VICTIM

1. The First Victim 9
2. The First Opinion 18
3. Dead Man 26
4. Dimmock's Ride 35
5. Inquest 46

Book II
THE VILLAGE OF SILENCE

6. A Report for Dr Palfrey 53
7. Matt Stone 62
8. Visitors to Conne 72
9. Snap Decision 82
10. The Cottage 95
11. Defiance 107
12. The Squad 114
13. Kathleen O'Shea 124
14. Larsen 136
15. The One Voice 147
16. Ring of Fire 156
17. The Ordeal 163
18. The Ultimatum 167

Book III
THE PLAGUE

19. The Attack 179
20. The Escape 184
21. The Plant 190
22. Night of Dread 199
23. Rondivallo 209

BOOK I

THE FIRST VICTIM

1. The First Victim

IT was not known until long afterwards, and in fact she had only a small place in the official records, but little Jane Hill was the first victim in England.

Larry Hill slowed down as he drew near the cottage on his bicycle, and waited with unashamed eagerness for a movement at a window or at the back door. He was on time, and Jane was usually on the look-out for him. This evening there was no sign of her. He gave a little grimace, told himself that it was absurd to be disappointed, and swung his leg off the bicycle as the front wheel drew within an inch of the newly-painted green gate. Everything about the cottage looked fresh and attractive—woodwork, brasswork, windows, even the tiles, although in fact they were over two hundred years old. At the back there was a patch of them which Larry had not yet cleaned; it would be the last job of renovating the cottage in the three years since they had bought it.

He whistled a song, quite sure that in a moment Jane would appear, at window, door or corner; little Jane, who looked absurdly young to be a married woman with a four-year-old son.

Suddenly, Larry caught his breath.

Young James was spending a week with his grandmother, having a seaside holiday in perfect weather, and with three days still to go. Surely nothing had happened at Bournemouth?

Of course not; Jane would never have gone off without telling him, or sending a message. The office people would always pass a message through to the men in the warehouse and on deliveries. It was absurd to worry, and also absurd to think that the idyll would go on for ever. But he longed to see Jane, with her fair hair and bright eyes and the complexion which looked almost too perfect. An art dealer in the town had once said that she belonged on a chocolate box, but he didn't know how she glowed with vitality.

Larry reached the corner of the cottage, wheeling the bicycle, frowning now because all but the birds were silent. Behind him was the lawn which he had cut last night, and the flower beds filled with antirrhinums only just beginning to flower; Jane's planting. Hers was the flower garden, his the lawns and the vegetables. He did not even glance at the rows of peas in flower, the sturdy scarlet runners already knee-high, the beds of onions, carrots and potatoes in their half acre. He lodged the old black bicycle against the shed which housed it, the firewood, logs and most of the things they stored. He went towards the back door with its small tiled porch. The ladder still stood against the corner, and he planned to get up on the roof for a couple of hours tonight. By the weekend the job would be finished; the realisation of a golden dream.

The back door was closed, although on an evening in early summer Jane usually had it open, for the late sun came in. This was Tuesday; ironing day.

Larry opened the door and stepped into the kitchen: the brightness of stainless steel, of tiles, of everything as modern as it could be except for the big smokeless fuel stove, one of the earliest type, which he intended to replace soon. They'd have more money to spare now that the main work was done.

Jane had been ironing.

A chair was close to the ironing board, and over a big clothes horse their clothes were draped, dazzling white as the sun poured upon them. A pile of clothes waiting to be ironed lay in a heap on the kitchen table; mostly his underwear. The electric iron stood on end, as if Jane had left all this in a hurry. In fact it was just as it would have been had she known it was him coming, and had jumped up to go and meet him.

The kitchen door was open.

This led into the one large downstairs room, with its small windows, its two ancient oak beams, its old fireplace; that fireplace had been the thing which had made them decide to buy the cottage. Now it was surrounded by burnished brasses and gleaming copper pieces; it was the Hills' boast that nothing in this room was less than a hundred years old, and much of the furniture was Tudor.

Larry stepped across the uneven wooden floor, with its three skin rugs, to the door in the corner which led to the stairs and the front door.

It was almost dark there; little daylight reached the old staircase.

"Jane!" Larry called.

There was no answer.

Uneasily, he began to climb the stairs. It did not seriously occur to him that he might find Jane in trouble here, and his hazy thoughts were all about young James, the possibility that a message hadn't reached him, even that he'd passed Jane on the way. He reached the little square landing. Here were three rooms: the child's bedroom, theirs, and the tiny bathroom. Neither of the bedrooms was big, but both were big enough. The bathroom was an amateur's triumph; practically everything had been done by Larry and Jane: even the plumbing. He'd had it checked by a friend at the factory, and it had been fully approved.

Larry looked into their bedroom, the door of which was ajar.

"I wish to goodness I knew—" he began, and then stopped abruptly, for he thought he heard a sound. He swung round, and his face cleared.

11

"Is that you, Jane?"

There was no answer and no repetition of the sound, which had been rather like a muted cry. Perhaps she was hurrying back along the road, having misjudged the time. He had to remind himself that it was crazy to think that she would always be waiting on the very tick of six o'clock.

He heard the sound again, and realized that it was nearer than he had first thought. He strode out and into the boy's room.

No. Empty.

He heard the sound again, undoubtedly a little strangled cry, and thrust open the bathroom door, feeling a choky kind of fear.

There was Jane, lying on the floor. Her eyes were wide open, staring at him, her lips were working.

He went swift as a hawk towards her and dropped on his knees, saying in a hoarse, frightened voice: "Janey, what is it, what's happened?" It was an accident of some kind. She'd hurt her back. Oh God, she'd hurt her back! What must he do? Be careful, don't move her too much until he was sure what had happened. How had it happened? What did that matter?

There she lay, with his hands upon her now, in her silent fear.

"Janey, what is it?" he asked desperately. "Where does it hurt?"

Her mouth worked, and he knew that she was trying to answer but could not. *She could not speak*. It was some kind of stroke, some kind of paralysis of the throat, too. In her eyes was fear of unnamed things. She tried to get up, but there was no strength in her.

"Don't try to move," Larry said. "Just nod or shake your head. Are you hurt?" She shook her head a fraction. No? "Did you fall?" she shook her head again. "Can't you move?" Lunatic question, and she shook her head. But did she really know what he was asking? "Am I hurting you?" He was feeling gently over her arms,

12

her legs, then slid a hand beneath her back and ran his fingers along the spine; everything seemed normal, and she kept shaking her head with a fractional movement, as if even that was more than she could do. She was deathly pale, and her eyes unusually bright, but there were no outward signs of injury or of sickness.

Paralysis . . . ?

"I'm going to lift you and carry you to the bed," Larry said very carefully. "If I hurt you, close your eyes, and I'll know." With infinite care he slid both arms beneath her and lifted. She did not close her eyes as he carried her into the bedroom with its low ceiling, its oak rafters, the big double bed, the uneven, creaking floor. Habit was a strange thing: for a moment he was tempted to hold her with one arm and turn back the bedspread with his free hand; but he did not; just laid her down gently.

"Listen, Janey," he said carefully, "I'm going to ask one of the Carters to come and wait with you, and then I'm going to the village. I'll telephone Dr Dimmock, and I know he'll come just as soon as he can. One of the Carters will be here in ten minutes, too, so don't worry. Understand?"

She nodded. But there was something in her expression which he didn't understand, as if she was pleading for something. Then her lips moved and she made a little sound, a kind of whimpering. What did she want? What——

Fool. *Water!*

"Water?"

She nodded.

Crazy fool. Of course she wanted water. What about some brandy? There was no reason why he shouldn't give her brandy, was there? First he fetched water and held the glass to her lips, but she could not drink, and he had to tip the glass slightly. He saw a fluttering movement at her throat as she tried to swallow, but even that seemed too much for her.

"I'm going to get you a spot of brandy," he said, and

13

straightened up. Then he heard the sound of a car engine not far off. His eyes lit up. "That'll be Dave Carter! I'll be back in two shakes."

He swung round and went headlong down the stairs, ducking because the ceiling was too low for his six feet, ducking again beneath the front-door lintel as he went out. He shouted when he saw the old Austin, the only car which passed the cottage regularly: this was a dead-end road. Only tradespeople came down, apart from the Hills and the Carters, and they came mostly during the day. The car was a fifteen-year-old model, useful for the little market garden work the Carters did; but its noisy engine might drown all cries.

"*Dave!*" Larry bellowed. "Dave!" and went tearing towards the gate. It was just possible that Carter wouldn't notice him, but usually he looked this way, to wave if anyone was about. "*Dave!*" Larry shrieked, and the car jolted. Carter glanced round as if in surprise and alarm, and the car slowed down.

"Hallo, Larry, is something the matter?" Carter was a slow-speaking man in the middle fifties, balding, strong and weather-beaten.

"Dave, Jane's—Jane's had some kind of a stroke. She can't move or speak, she——" Hill had to pause for breath as he opened the gate. "Can you—take me into the village so that I can—phone Dr Dimmock?"

"I certainly can," Carter said, and proved that his slowness of speech was no indication of the speed with which his mind could work. "Is anyone with Jane now?"

"No, I wondered if you——"

"The best thing to do," said Carter with great understanding, "is for you to take the car, Larry, and go into the village. I'll go and see how Jane is. If she's not too bad, I'll take your bike and go and fetch Mabel. You need a woman there." He was already getting out of the little car; standing upright, he was scarcely higher than Larry's shoulder. "Don't worry too much, Larry, these things often aren't so bad as they seem."

"No," Larry said gruffly. The important thing was the car. "Thanks, Dave, thanks a lot." He got into the car and drove to a patch of grass where he could turn; driving was second nature to him, for he was always at the wheel of a Wide World Food van. "Thanks, Dave!" he called again, as he passed the gateway. Carter was already halfway towards the open front door.

Now all that mattered was getting hold of Dr Dimmock. Dimmock wasn't due to visit Conne, the village, until the day after tomorrow; his home and surgery were in Lauriston, twelve miles away. He might be out on his rounds now, or at a surgery, anywhere.

If not Dimmock, then who?

"Cross that stream when I get to it," Larry muttered. He saw the village church with its square grey tower only a mile ahead, and the roofs of the houses just beyond. A telephone box was outside the little post office in the middle of the village. Larry slowed down. Children were playing, men and women were already busy in their gardens, two farm horses stood beneath the shade of an oak tree, with their great handsome heads over a gateway. The sun was warm but it wasn't too hot; a perfect summer's day, with everything quite normal.

Had he coppers for the prepayment box?

Yes.

He gave the number, still in a kind of ferment. First a child answered; then a woman with a curt voice who said she wasn't sure whether the doctor was in. Who wanted him? If he held on, she would find out. Disapproval and pessimism were in the tone of her voice, it was almost possible to believe that she was resentful. Then came the thing Larry had almost given up hoping for: Dr Dimmock's deep voice.

"Hallo, Larry Hill," the doctor greeted. "I thought it was time I had another call from you, but I expected it to be from your wife."

What the devil was he talking about?

15

"Doctor, can you possibly come and see my wife right away? She's had some kind of a stroke, and can't move or speak. I just got home and found her."

"Steady a moment," Dr Dimmock said in a brisker voice. "Now, tell me more about it."

There was so much and yet so little to tell, and every word took precious time.

"I don't know what to make of it, but don't worry, it doesn't sound too bad," Dimmock said. "I can't come myself, but I think my colleague can, I'll make sure that he's in. Hold on." Dimmock went off the line, and Larry leaned against the side of the kiosk, taking out his handkerchief and wiping his forehead, then licking his lips. He felt sick as he waited, and Dimmock seemed to be an age.

In fact it was only two or three minutes before he spoke again.

"You there, Hill? . . . Yes, Dr Korven will come out at once, and I think you'd better meet him by the village Post office, or he'll lose his way."

Thank God!

"I'll wait here myself," Larry said, huskily. "I—I can't thank you enough, doctor."

"No need to thank me for anything," Dr Dimmock said, "but there's one thing you ought to know. Dr Korven is my new assistant, but sometimes patients are a little surprised to find a coloured doctor. You can place absolute reliance on Dr Korven, though."

"Provided he's a doctor and he's coming straight away, nothing else matters," Larry said.

"He'll be on his way in five minutes," Dr Dimmock promised. "If I were you, I'd go across the road to the Wheatsheaf and have a drink. It will make waiting easier, and you sound as if you could do with a pick-me-up."

That was so like Dimmock.

"Good idea, doctor," Larry said, "I will. Thank you again, I really am grateful."

16

He rang off, and stared along the winding road towards Lauriston, estimating that this Dr Korven would take at least twenty minutes to get here. A coloured man. What did that mean? A Negro, or an Indian?

What did it matter?

All that mattered was getting Jane better.

If she got worse . . .

Larry had a whisky and soda, was chaffed by two of the villagers because he seldom came into the Wheatsheaf, told them what had brought him, and that Dr Korven was on his way. No one had yet seen Korven, but a farmhand said almost casually:

"Did hear Dr Dimmock was getting past it, like, and he'd taken on an assistant, one of these black fellers. It's a changing world, that's what I have to say, things are a lot different from what they were in my young days."

"You had to work for a living then, instead of sitting your backside on a tractor," the barman said as two more customers came in.

Larry finished his drink and went outside; the flat, unemotional voices got on his nerves. A quarter of an hour had passed, and he could soon start looking along the road.

It was another twleve minutes before the sound of a motor cycle or a Vespa became audible, and there was still no car in sight. Larry looked towards the church and three miles beyond, to the cottage and Jane. If this damned doctor didn't hurry, he'd have to go and see Jane himself; one of the chaps in the Wheatsheaf would direct the doctor to the cottage.

The little motor cycle sounded louder, then stopped alongside the car. A youthful-looking man with a face as black as coal stared at Larry with questioning eyes and a hint of a smile.

Larry's heart leapt.

"Dr Korven?"

"That is right." The man's voice was very deep and the words were uttered slowly.

"Will you just follow me?" Larry asked. "Or would you rather come in the car?"

"I will follow you," said Dr Korven. "Not too fast, please."

2.   The First Opinion

MABEL CARTER was with Jane.

Larry saw the change of expression on her plump, flabby face when she first saw Dr Korven. She wasn't a woman he particularly liked, and he had often seen her tight-lipped, like this, whenever she disapproved of anything or anyone; and she was a specialist in disapproval. Dr. Korven inclined his head to her, smiled gravely, and said:

"Perhaps you will tell me what you have done to help the patient, Mrs Carter."

"I've done all a sensible person could do," said Mabel, tartly. "I've kept her warm, and kept moistening her lips. I gave her one spoonful of brandy, but that didn't seem to do any good, and she didn't want any more."

"I see," said Dr Korven. "I will be glad if you will assist me, please."

Mrs Carter nodded.

Larry could only think of Jane, who lay on her back with two eiderdowns taken out of winter storage and piled on her. She looked paler than ever, although she must be so hot. Her curly fair hair was like a child's on the wine red of the bedspread.

"May I stay?" Larry asked, chokily.

"If you wish," said Korven.

It was strange to see his dark hands against Jane's whiteness. He was deliberate and yet wholly impersonal, and did exactly what Larry would have expected

18

Dimmock to do. Stethoscope, a pencil torch to see inside the mouth, tapping at the knees to try to get a reaction; all this in complete silence, while Mrs Carter looked on with that obvious but unspoken disapproval.

Larry wondered what Dr Korven thought about it.

The Mrs Carters of this world would always object to anything new, but he had worked with coloured men and had come almost to forget their colour. Certainly he wasn't concerned with the colour of Korven's skin just then; was concerned only with a doctor's findings. Korven said so little that it was almost frightening; and he seemed both serious and absorbed as he studied Jane's arms and shoulders, and touched her right arm near a little red swelling.

"Are there many mosquitoes near here?" he asked.

"There's an old pond near the mill, I'm always asking the council to clean it out," Mrs Carter said. "Can't sleep for the little brutes some nights."

Dr Korven nodded, looked for other spots but found none, and stood back from the bed.

He smiled at Mrs Carter, saying:

"You were very good, Mrs Carter, it is so important to keep the patient warm. Are you able to stay with Mrs Hill, or do your domestic duties require you?"

"Well, if she needs constant nursing, I can't manage it."

"For the time being all that Mrs Hill needs is the company of friends," Korven said, and turned to look at his stricken woman on the bed. His smile, with the white teeth dazzling, seemed to bring brightness and hope into the room. "I do not know what has happened to cause your general physical condition, Mrs Hill, apart from the signs you know about. I can tell you some things: for instance, it is not poliomyelitis."

Larry thought: "Thank God," and felt weak with a wave of relief.

"It is not a heart condition either. There is a slight

19

swelling in the throat, both inside and outside, which I do not understand, but the prostration could be caused by shock." He smiled reassuringly, and glanced at Larry. "Yes, it could be caused by shock, and we are at a disadvantage because your wife cannot talk. That is why I am going to ask some questions. She will perhaps answer with a nod or a shake of the head."

"That's how I questioned her." Larry was eager.

"Don't you think she ought to rest?" demanded Mrs Carter aggressively.

"I do indeed," said Korven. "But there are some facts we ought to know first in order to help her. It may take a little time to find them."

"I think I'll go and see how things are at home, and come back later," Mrs Carter said. "And if she really wants a day and night nurse, I really couldn't manage."

"Why don't you arrange for Mr Hill to send for you if he needs your help?" suggested Korven.

Larry thought: "He wants to get rid of her." He felt a measure of relief when Mrs Carter agreed to go, and saw her to the head of the stairs. She leaned close to him and whispered:

"I'm not prejudiced, but the sooner you get Dr Dimmock in person to come and see her, the better it will be. That's if you want *my* opinion."

"I hope he'll be here soon," Larry said, and that seemed to satisfy her.

He went back to the bedroom, to see Korven standing by the foot of the bed, the stethoscope and other instruments back in the case, the case closed. He was dressed in a suit of clerical grey, immaculately cut, and obviously was only in his early twenties. His round head was a cluster of close black curls, and his dark skin showed up vividly against his white collar, shirt and cuffs.

Jane was looking more relaxed, as if some of the tension had eased; certainly no one could have been more soothing than this doctor.

"Now we will try," Korven said.

He asked the questions gently. Had she received a great shock? No. Had she seen anything frightening? No. Had she fallen down and banged her head? No. Had she bumped her head against a cupboard, a door, anything hard? No. Each "no" was just a little sideways movement of her head on the pillow, as Larry sat by the side of the bed, watching tensely.

Had she received any kind of electric shock? No.

The deep voice brought out question after question clearly, and Korven seemed to know exactly what he was driving at.

Had the feeling of paralysis first started in her legs? No. Arms? No. Throat?

Yes!

Larry felt a surge of excitement as Jane nodded, and did not notice anything different about the movement of her head. But Korven did. He seemed startled, stared very intently, for a moment almost frighteningly. Then he asked in the same measured tones:

"Was it a soreness?"

"No."

"Stiffness?"

"Yes."

"Had it come suddenly?"

"Yes."

"Very quickly?"

His questions elicited the fact that it had taken about ten minutes to get to its worst; and at its worst Jane had hardly been able to breath. Some details weren't yet known, but at least the important facts seemed to be: this trouble had started in her throat and spread to the rest of her body.

"Now, please, will you nod your head quickly, three or four times," Korven asked.

Jane nodded, not vigorously but quite quickly, and as she did so Larry thought that her movements were much more free than they had been. A choky kind of excitement made him shiver. Jane realised the difference too, and began to nod and then to shake her head and to try to move her arms underneath the eiderdown; there was some movement there as well as at her feet.

"I think I will wait to see how you get on now," Dr Korven said. "If you don't mind, Mr Hill, I will have a walk in your beautiful garden."

"Oh, of course!" Larry said. He went to the door to let the coloured doctor go out, then sprang to the bed and gripped Jane's hands, which lay outside the eiderdown.

"It's all right darling, you're getting better, you're going to be all right!" He was shrill with excitement.

Jane's eyes were very bright. She could move her lips, and Larry tried to lip-read but could not understand. It didn't really matter.

"Anything you'd like?" he asked.

A nod.

"More water?"

A nod.

"I'll get some right away," Larry said, and hurried for a glass of cool, fresh water, came back and held it to her lips. This time she drank slowly, and there was noticeably less evidence of paralysis.

Larry put the glass down and went to the window, partly to conceal the tears in his eyes. He saw Dr Korven sitting on one of the posts of the fence, relaxed in the evening sun and apparently contented. Three boys, two of the Carter children and a cousin, all aged about nine or ten, came cycling along the path which ran alongside the garden, and as they passed the doctor two of them put out their tongues.

The little brutes!

Korven's expression did not alter. He took out a cigarette and lit it, still staring into the distance.

It was an unpleasant incident, and coming on top of Mrs Carter's advice, made it clear how deep prejudice went. Well he, Larry Hill, couldn't do anything about it.

He turned back to Jane.

She was hitching herself up in bed.

"Janey, be careful!"

When he tried to stop her she made a face at him. Soon she was sitting nearly upright against the pillows. Her colour was better and her lips were no longer pale. Her smile came quite freely, and it seemed obvious that before long she would be herself again.

When Dr Korven came up, he said: "It is not surprising that as the stiffness began in the throat, it will leave the throat last, also. Mrs Hill, I must tell you most seriously that you must rest. We do not know what caused this brief affliction, but we know that you have had a severe shock, and, rest is essential. Can that be arranged here?"

"We can arrange it. My sister will come," Larry said confidently. "I'll handle things until she does; I can take tomorrow off." He felt that glow of excitement, even though one part of his mind seemed to say: "You're a sentimental idiot." Well, why not? He was in love, wasn't he? Five years married, and Jane mattered as much as ever.

"It may be wise to have a nurse here for a night or two. I will consult Dr Dimmock and arrange it if he agrees."

Anything, so long as it helped to make sure that Janey got well quickly.

"Do not make any attempt to force the recovery of the power of speech," went on Dr Korven. "I shall come again later in the evening and bring a soothing lotion which will perhaps help. Remember, do not try to make yourself talk. Stay in bed. Eat only very soft foods. Milk broth, perhaps; or soup would be best, or fish. Are you hungry?"

Jane nodded; and her eyes were brimming over with a kind of merriment. You couldn't keep Janey down for long!

"She eats more than I do, although she's still only

eight-stone-four," Larry said. "Doctor, I can't thank you enough."

"I have done nothing," Dr Korven said. "I am anxious only to know how long it is before her voice comes back. The time is very important." He picked up his small black case and moved towards the door, smiling round at Jane.

She formed two words carefully: "Thank you."

Downstairs, Larry said earnestly: "Is there anything you preferred not to tell my wife, doctor?"

"I have little more to say," said Korven. "Your wife has had a rare infection of the throat, and undoubtedly will have to be kept under observation, but it will be better if she believes Dr Dimmock has arranged for a nurse." He gave his bright, attractive smile. "I will tell you more when I come back with the nurse."

"When will that be?"

"I shall be here at ten o'clock," the doctor told him. "I shall know my way, there is no need to come and meet me."

"I wonder——" Larry began, and then said: "Oh, it doesn't matter."

"What would you like me to do?"

"Well, if you could phone a telegram to my sister, it would get there some time tonight. I'm sure she'll be here by midday tomorrow."

"Please write down the message and I will arrange it." Dr Korven promised.

Ten minutes later Larry saw the Vespa moving steadily towards Conne. The three children were on the road, fooling about with their bicycles; he hoped they weren't lying in wait for the doctor. It was too far away to be able to see their faces, so he turned back to Jane.

"My goodness, you gave me a scare," he said. "But it's only a matter of time, now."

She nodded, and formed words with her lips.

"Don't try to talk," Larry said hastily. "The doctor was

emphatic about that. Don't try, just let nature take its course."

Jane nodded again.

Larry went downstairs to get supper, and decided on scrambled eggs and milk broth to follow, for them both; that would be the easy way, and he could finish with plenty of bread and cheese. He was about twenty minutes, and when he went into the bedroom with the tray, he had a sneaking hope that Jane would be able to speak, if only in a whisper.

But she could not.

He wondered, if Dr Korven did know more than he had said; whether he had known that it would be some time before she got her voice back; what he had meant by "rare".

At least Jane had enjoyed her supper!

Larry moved the radio up into the bedroom, where it could stay for a few days, then went to wash up. He wondered if Dr Korven had sent that telegram; whether he had talked to Dimmock; whether he would be here at ten o'clock. Larry did not seriously doubt it; Korven had impressed him as a reliable man in every way. But was Dr Dimmock wise to have him as a partner in a country district like this, where only white people lived? Dimmock was known to be a man of strong opinions, stubborn and sometimes obstinate. Not that it was his, Larry Hill's, business.

It was dark at half-past nine.

At ten, Larry fancied that he heard the noise of the Vespa engine, but he was mistaken, the noise didn't get any louder; the wind was probably carrying sounds from the main road, two miles away.

At ten-past ten Larry was surprised that Korven hadn't arrived.

By half-past, when there was still no sign of the doctor, he was acutely disappointed.

To make it worse, Jane still couldn't utter a word.

25

3. Dead Man

Dr Wilberforce Abraham Korven had every intention of going back to Vale Cottage, and did not intend to be alone. Nothing of his inward excitement showed as he drove off or as he passed the boys. They stared rudely, but made no gestures and did not call out. The narrow road had a single strip of tar, just wide enough for a car. He kept up a good speed, trying to decide whether to stop at the Wheatsheaf and telephone to London, or whether to go home to his lodgings in Lauriston. Lauriston had an automatic exchange, and it would be safer to talk from there.

It wouldn't take long: half an hour would make little difference.

But it could be fatal. When he had come down here, Palfrey had told him to report any discovery at once, had impressed him with the urgency.

Palfrey . . .

The good man, the great man, one of the few who really seemed unaware of the colour of a man's skin.

Korven slowed down near the post-office, then saw a girl in the telephone box and an elderly man waiting as if to make a call. That decided Korven. He put his foot down and shot past the low Tudor buildings and along the narrow, winding High Street. Two people watched him from a cottage door, and at the last house in the village, where a child played on the narrow pavement, a woman called:

"Elsa, mind that motor-bike!"

The wind carried the warning and the fear to Korven, and he slowed down. He was calm again now that the decision had been made for him. It would be far better to talk freely to Palfrey than to guard his words.

There were only two small villages between here and Lauriston. Hampshire was a much larger country than he had realized before he had come to work with Dimmock, on Palfrey's recommendation. Dimmock: there was a man, too. But Korven did not think very much about the old doctor, he was concentrating on speed, eager to tell Palfrey that he had found this peculiar throat affliction and the paralytic condition.

The road ahead was winding and in places there were steep hills; it was not easy for speed.

He noticed a car parked just off the road at the entrance to a field, passed it, then saw it moving after him, reflected in his driving mirror. It was a big, old car; perhaps a taxi. It should soon pass him. Instead, it followed slowly, even when there was a long straight stretch of road ahead. There was the forest, too: the Forest of Conne, where the road ran through massed trees, and where even at midsummer it was dark and shady; this evening it was cool. There was a mile-long tunnel formed by the interlocking branches of ancient beech trees on either side of the road.

The car was about fifty yards behind when he reached the forest, and the sun showed only as a distant tracery of light. The leaves of beech, birch and oak looked almost translucent, and there was much beauty on either side, with small clearings and great trees, little glades, narrow footpaths, here and there parking places.

The car behind Korven was hidden by a bend in the road, but it came in sight again, travelling much faster.

"It can't be after me," he muttered. "No one knows me."

He couldn't hope to outpace the car, so he pulled over to allow it plenty of room. His mirror showed two young men in the front, and he thought he saw a third, behind them. They couldn't be after him, but—Palfrey had warned him how dangerous this task might be: how deadly, too.

The car was about to overtake.

It was very close.

He felt a choking fear, for it was so close that he could almost touch it. He pulled further over, on to the grass verge: the front wheel wobbled. Then the car passed, swung in front of him and jolted to a standstill. He could not avoid banging into the back, but was travelling so slowly that the collision did not hurt him or the Vespa. He was frightened as he trundled the machine on to the grass, and two young men came hurrying from the front of the car.

He had never seen either of them before.

He must not say a word to let them think he had been half prepared for this.

They came hurrying, one on either side of the Vespa, as if to make sure that he couldn't get away. One man had a narrow face with thin lips and a spiteful look; the other might have been anyone in a crowd.

Korven propped the machine up as they drew level, still on either side of him.

"The one thing you must never do, in any circumstances, is name me or Z5," Palfrey had said. *"You are one of us because we believe you would be prepared to die rather than betray Z5."*

It had seemed so easy to promise.

Now, it was almost impossible to behave as if he did not guess what these men wanted.

"Do you know you nearly caused a serious accident?" He was sharp-voiced.

They didn't even speak, just set upon him. He had no chance to defend himself. One man struck him in the stomach, the other on the jaw, and as he swayed helplessly, he felt a thudding blow on the back of the head, and lost consciousness.

When he came round he was aware of pain in his head, and a different kind of pain at his wrists and ankles. At first he did not understand; but then he remembered. He tried to open his eyes but could not, and it was so dark that he thought he was blind. Then he realized that something was tied round his head, blinding him, and that his wrists and his ankles were bound too. He felt a smooth, steady motion, and realized that he was propped up in the corner of a car.

Was it that old "taxi"?

Fear was less acute now, partly because he was still dazed. He did not stir, except to try to ease the constriction at his wrists, but he could not do it. He smelt tobacco smoke, sweet and pleasant.

Soon he began to wriggle about, and no one took any notice.

The car slowed down.

The one thing you must never do is to name me or Z5.

He felt the car turn a corner and then climb a steep hill, and soon he realized that the surface was nothing like so good as it had been. The car bumped. The driver changed gear; once, twice. Then they bumped to a standstill, and there was a noticeable squeak as the handbrake went on. Korven heard movements first inside the car, then outside. A door opened.

Fear was coming back, greater now.

On his very first job for Z5, this happened.

A man from outside the car said: "Got him?"

"Yes."

"Any trouble?"

"Just started to fidget."

"He talked?"

"Chance would be a fine thing."

"We got rid of the Vespa," the newcomer said. "Drove it right over. It'll be in little pieces on those rocks."

There was a chuckle; low-pitched, ugly; that did more than anything else to turn Korven's fear to a kind of terror, and he began to shiver.

One of the men went on;

"There'll soon be another thing in little pieces."

Korven could not stop himself from trembling, yet his mind worked swiftly, every tiny detail of what they said and did impressed itself on his mind. They lit cigarettes, moved about outside the car, spoke occasionally, and gave the impression that they were waiting for something or someone. Then there was the sound of a car engine some way off, which drew nearer.

"This'll be him," one of the men said.

Him?

Korven was pulling at the cords at his wrists and straining at those at his ankles, but he couldn't shift any. The darkness seemed to make his situation worse. He heard footsteps on the rough ground, then one of these two men said:

"That you, Mr Smith?"

A man said in a thin voice: "Yes. Is he here?"

"Safe as houses."

"Let me see him," the newcomer said. The tone of authority was very noticeable.

The door opened wider and Korven felt hands at his legs; another door opened and hands pulled at his shoulders. He was half lifted, half dragged out, but he couldn't stand upright, the men on either side saved him from falling. He fought for courage and tried to picture Palfrey's fine, calm face, to hear his quiet, confident voice.

"Push him against a tree," said the man named Smith.

"Right."

"You needn't be gentle."

They weren't gentle.

Korven leaned against a tree, and one man still held his wrists. Hands plucked at the cloth round his eyes, and he felt a bandage being taken off. There were several layers. At last he could see a pale glow, but there was no bright light even when the last layer had been peeled off.

Gradually the night took shape. There were trees, two of the men, the car, a better light some distance off, with a shimmery look about it. The sun had set behind a bank of clouds and was lighting up the edges of the cloud. He was still in the forest: or in a forest. Then he was aware of something else: light shimmered as on water, and there was a faint roaring sound.

They were close to the sea; and they had talked of driving the Vespa right over.

A man spoke from his side.

"You're Dr Korven, partner to Dr Dimmock of Lauriston. That right?"

"Yes," Korven managed to say. "Yes, that is right, why are you behaving like this?"

"Just answer my questions. Who sent you to see Mrs Hill?"

"Dimmock did."

"What did he tell you?"

"He—he just said that Mrs Hill had been paralysed, he could not go himself and wanted me to see her. That is all, I cannot understand why——"

"If you start making a speech you'll get badly hurt. Did Dimmock say anything else?"

"No."

"He give you any special instructions?"

"How could he do that, he did not know what was the matter with this woman!"

"He tell you what you might expect to find?"

"Listen to me, please," said Korven, pleadingly. "This is the simple truth: he told me that Mr Hill had telephoned about his wife, who had had some kind of stroke. He could not go to see her, because tonight he had to see another patient. Also, it was his night off. So he asked me to go. He promised to go himself if I thought that wise. He told me that Mrs Hill was an attractive young woman, with one child. That she was very strong but also very small, and that I was not to be

31

deceived by her smallness. She was intelligent, also. That is all Dr Dimmock told me."

"Did he suggest any kind of treatment?"

"He could not, he did not know what was wrong." Korven was sweating freely, and his voice kept breaking; for he feared that death was very near, and its nearness was worse because it seemed so purposeless. Why was this happening? Why had he——

"Ever heard the name of Palfrey?" asked the man whose name was Smith.

Oh, God.

The one thing you must never do is to name me, or Z5.

"I—I do not understand you."

"Palfrey, spelt like a kind of horse. P A L F R E Y. *Palfrey.*"

Korven gasped.

"No. No, I do not know the name."

"Know anyone named Sap?"

Sap Palfrey.

"No!"

"Bruton?"

"No."

"Do you know Andromovitch?"

Stefan, the Russian.

"Please," Korven said desperately, "I know none of these people. I have done nothing, I assure you, let me go now, I have to see Dr Dimmock about my patient, she is very sick."

"You needn't worry any more about your patient, she'll be looked after." That was sneered. "Did you telephone Dimmock from the village?"

"No."

"That's right, he didn't," a man said.

All this time they had been standing behind Korven, as if they did not intend to let him see clearly, but now the man called Smith stepped in front of him, and stood

32

only a yard away. The fading light shone on his heavy-featured face, and there was no sign of kindness or goodness. He was tall and bulky. The others were still behind Korven, who leaned back against the tree, trying to control a fit of shivering.

"Listen to me," Smith said. "Remember that if you tell any lies you won't live to see the night out. This patient, the woman Hill: what was she suffering from?"

"I do not know."

"Ever seen anyone like it before?"

He had come to look for such a seizure, and Palfrey had described the signs *exactly*.

"Not the same way, no. She was paralysed. It appears to have started from a throat infection."

A man out of sight caught his breath; it was like a wince. The bulky Smith didn't change his expression, but raised one hand sharply, as if the words "throat infection" had some special significance.

"How do you know it started from the throat?" he demanded softly.

"I asked her."

Swift as a whip, the man's arm moved, and his finger slapped savagely on Korven's face.

"You're lying, you couldn't question her, she couldn't talk."

"No," Korven gasped in despairing agreement. "She couldn't talk, but when I asked questions she nodded her head, that's the way she answered. I have told you all the truth, all of it. Please believe me."

The man named Smith said almost casually:

"I believe you have, too. Okay, boys, let him go."

Let him go seemed to flare like a great flame in Korven's mind. *Let him go*. He had fooled them! He need not have feared death, they were going to release him, there was no need to worry. *Let him go*.

A man slashed the cords at his ankles. He was pushed forward, then hustled through the near darkness. The

33

others seemed to be able to see much better than he could. One man was behind him and another at his side, and the only sound was of their footsteps. His feet dragged, but they didn't let him rest. If they were going to let him go——

They weren't! He was wrong. He knew what that cryptic phrase meant: he was to be thrown over a cliff, on to the rocks, like the Vespa. He managed to break free, and plunged towards the right, away from the sea and the cliff. He could see the shape of the cliff against the afterglow now, could hear the hissing roaring of the sea, not far away. He tried to run, but could hardly see. He was blinded by his own fears as well as the darkness.

He must not name Palfrey.

He stumbled against the root of the tree and pitched forward, tried to save himself but could not. Then he felt the others pounce, lift him, and carry him bodily; all his struggles were of no avail. They reached the edge of the cliff, and he could see nothing but blackness, although he could hear waves smacking up against rocks below, as if they were calling out for him.

Then, he was struck on the back of the head.

He did not realize what was happening when they pitched him over.

"It's a good job Dimmock didn't go himself," said a man to Smith, "there'd have been a bit of fuss over him. No one will worry about what's happened to that black so-and-so."

"We shall have to watch Dimmock," Smith said evenly.

4. Dimmock's Ride

DR ARTHUR DIMMOCK climbed out of his car, outside the garage at the side of his house in the centre of Lauriston, and opened the front door of the house as his wife stepped from the car. He switched on a light and was revealed as a short, stocky man with silvery grey hair; his wife looked taller and much slimmer.

"You get in, dear, won't keep you a jiff," Dimmock said. "Expect there'll be a message from Korven. I may have to go out to Conne."

"Oh, Arthur, not tonight."

"Doctors can't be choosers," Dimmock said, aware that he had said that at least once on every day of his life since he had passed his examinations, and he gave a little perky smile. He had an Irish look about him, an Irish merriness in his voice and manner, although his voice was quite free from accent. I'll see if the Vespa is at the back."

His wife went in as Dimmock opened the garage doors. There was no Vespa, just two old bicycles, a narrow work bench, two inner tubes patched and waiting until they came in useful, and a few oddments. He stamped to the house itself, where his wife had put on more lights, and stepped into a spacious hall, carpeted from wall to wall. It had not only spaciousness but charm.

The door to his surgery was on the right of the hall, and there was another door to it leading from the side of the house; that was the way that Korven usually came in. Dimmock went in briskly, switching on two lights. He looked at the small desk where he made out his prescriptions and his National Health certificates, and did the other clerical work which sometimes exasperated him to furious protests. There were no messages on it. He sat on the corner of the desk, lifted the telephone and gave a number, swinging his right leg; it was a quarter to eleven. A woman answered.

"Oh, Nurse Windleham, Dr Dimmock here."

"Am I glad you're back!" exclaimed the woman. "I've had a terrible evening doctor. Dr Korven hasn't been in touch with me at all. I've tried to reach him at his home, but they say he hasn't been in all the evening. There were three urgent cases, I just *had* to refer to Dr Hardy." She was full of reproach; that Dimmock should have an evening off: that Korven should be trusted so much: that it was necessary to refer patients to another doctor.

"*Korven not back?*" Dimmock almost exploded. "Positive there's no message?"

"Good gracious me, doctor, I wouldn't tell you a thing like that if it wasn't true."

"All right, all right," said Dimmock testily. "Most peculiar business, though. He went out to an emergency call."

"You told me he'd gone to see Mrs Hill, out at Conne."

"That's right," said Dimmock. "All right, nurse, my wife will be in now, she'll take any more calls if I'm not here. Thank you for sitting in for me. Goodnight." He was brusque partly because it was his natural manner, partly because he was puzzled. He went out into the hall, leaving the lights blazing, and his wife came out of the drawing-room, patting her hair into position. She was very slim for a woman of over sixty, and looked a little tired. A few sequins sparkled in her black dress. "Hallo, dear. Funny kettle of fish. Korven's not been back, no message, nothing. I'll have to go and see what's the matter out at Conne."

"Oh, Arthur!"

"Like to come for the ride?" Dimmock asked, half

36

hopefully. He was at an age when long night drives on his own had no attraction. But his wife said:

"I don't see any reason why you should go unless you're called, and I certainly intend to go to bed."

"Hm, yes," said Dimmock. "Well, the quicker I'm off the quicker I'll be back." He gave her a peck of a kiss and went out, feeling a little uneasy, a little sorry about this: he had enjoyed the evening, would have enjoyed an hour in an armchair with the newspapers and a book, too. He gave rather a fierce little grin and went straight to the car. He didn't blame Gwen: she'd danced with a lot of the youngsters and was tired. Grandchildren didn't become twenty-one every day, though.

"But I can't understand it," Larry Hill said, looking at Dr Dimmock in the cottage's big downstairs room. "He left soon after seven o'clock and said he'd be back at ten."

"Hm, queer kettle of fish," grunted Dimmock. "Queer's certainly the word. Hope he's—well, never mind. Now I'm here I'll have a look at your wife, shall I?"

"Well, I don't know," Hill said. "She's just dropped off, doctor, and I don't want to disturb her."

"She all right now?"

"She seems all right, except that she hasn't got her voice back yet. It's beginning to worry her, and worry me, too. Dr Korven seemed so sure that she would be able to talk soon."

"Sorry, Larry," said Dimmock abruptly. "We'll have to wake her. I want to see this throat. I'll give her a dose that will send her to sleep afterwards, you needn't worry about that." He gripped Larry's forearm. "Never do to have a wife who couldn't tell you what she thinks of you, would it? Just imagine the number of men who dream and pray that their wives will lose their power of speech!"

37

Larry's smile was half-hearted.

At first Dimmock found nothing except a slight swelling and soreness to account for the continued loss of voice; and Jane Hill's general condition seemed as good as it could be. Then he saw a slight pale mark on her larynx, rather like the mark of some insect. Peculiar. He studied it as well as he could.

"Does your throat hurt?"

A shake of the head.

"Feel sore?"

Another shake.

"We'll see how it goes in the morning," Dimmock said. "Give her one of these tablets and a glass of hot milk, and she'll sleep like a top."

"What about her voice, doctor?" Larry asked.

"If she isn't back to normal by the morning, I'll get Dr Forsythe to have a look at her," Dimmock said. "Don't worry, Larry, I've never seen a fitter woman. The back of her mouth's a bit red and swollen. Could be . . . humph. No kidney troubles, no neglected illnesses, no arterial disease." He was muttering to himself. "Seems to be over the worst anyhow, probably get her voice back soon. Quite thought you were going to tell me that Number Two was on the way! Where's that strapping boy of yours?"

"He's with his grandmother in Bournemouth."

"Fine," said Dimmock. "Fine! Goodnight, and get a good sleep yourself."

Larry said: "Dr Korven said it would be wise to have a nurse. He said she must be kept under observation. I told my wife that. Don't you agree, doctor?"

"Can't say I do," said Dimmock. "Peculiar that he hasn't turned up. Be happier with a nurse?"

"Oh, no! But we'll need someone here. Do you know if Dr Korven sent that telegram for me?"

"Telegram?"

Larry explained.

Dimmock left soon afterwards with the address of Larry's sister in his pocket; he had promised to send a second telegram. He drove away slowly and thoughtfully, and as he approached Conne village, tried to imagine what could have happened to Korven. This was the first time there had been even the slightest suggestion of unreliability.

Dimmock had driven so many miles in all weathers along these narrow country roads that he gave little conscious thought to the task of driving. The beams of his headlamps slashed the summer darkness, rabbits' eyes showed a glistening pink, a fox crouched, staring. As he neared the village the green eyes of cats were turned towards him as if in secret malevolence. The lights reflected from the windows of the cottages and the inn, but the village was asleep and silent. One light showed in the top room of a small house on the outskirts. Still puzzled, a little drowsy, and beginning to think about his wife and the fact that he would soon have to retire, Dimmock neared the tunnel of trees through the forest. He knew the road well, was well aware of its eeriness. No one could ever drive through it alone, by night, without a feeling of tension.

Where the devil had Korven got to?

The headlights shone on trunks of trees and turned the leaves to a bright, silvery green. The sound of the car engine seemed louder here, as if the forest was shouting at him. Ahead, he saw the outline of a car pulled off the road. It was after one o'clock. Damned fools, to be out so late, thought Dimmock: couple of lovers probably, people were shameless about sex these days. As he drew nearer, travelling at nearly seventy miles an hour, he caught sight of the face of a man against the back window of the car. The face looked ghostlike in this fierce brightness, the eyes were half closed.

Dimmock muttered: "What the devil's all this?"

He eased his foot off the accelerator, then began to

apply the footbrake, not by any means sure of what he ought to do. He noticed the shadowy figure of another man on the far side of the car; and in some odd way, a shadow was cast on to the road, as if someone was crouching in front of the car.

At sixty-eight Arthur Dimmock had a mind as alert as a man half his age. He didn't like this situation at all. He would not have liked it had a man stood in front of the car, or at one side, to slow him down, and he suspected this furtiveness even more. He was travelling at about thirty miles an hour and was only thirty yards from the car.

Something peculiar had happened to Korven.

Suddenly, the crouching man in front of the other car stepped forward, hands raised and arms outstretched. The movement was so sudden that Dimmock jammed his foot hard on the brake. The man stepped right in front of the car, meaning to make absolutely sure that Dimmock did not pass.

He was waving, too.

The other car door opened and a second man got out. "Don't like it," Dimmock said in his gruff voice. "Damned if I do." He slowed down to fifteen miles an hour, and leaned sideways so that his voice would carry out of the open window: "What's all this about?"

He knew that it was a silly question. He also knew that it served his purpose, for the man in front moved to one side, so as to approach the window to talk, while the second man nipped to the other side of the road.

"Eh? What's wrong?" Dimmock demanded, in his gruffest, almost angry voice. "Breakdown? I'll telephone a garage for you."

Then he put his foot down on the accelerator and the car shot forward. The men on either side grabbed at it, but the shiny handles and the shiny doors slid off their fingers, and the car went from ten miles an hour to forty in twenty seconds. Dimmock caught a glimpse

40

of the men in the driving mirror while they were caught by the glow of his rear lights.

Then he saw a flash; a second and a third.

"Now I know I was right," he muttered with fierce satisfaction. "Shooting on the highway. Bloody murder!"

After another flash, he heard a sharp clang at the back of the car. It didn't do any harm, but meant that they were still within range. If they struck a tire, he'd have had it. Swine. Why the hell hadn't he fitted tubeless when he'd been advised to? Another flash: he almost winced, but this time there was no sound. The car travelling at over sixty miles an hour, the headlights were tunnelling through the forest where the road was so straight that there was no hope of getting out of sight quickly. Two miles or more, and there would be a series of sharp bends, where he could get further away. Ah!

He saw lights go on, and was sure that they were moving.

"Show *you*," he said, and there was a note almost of elation in his voice. Sixty-five, seventy, seventy-five. "Damn good job Mabel didn't come!" He laughed aloud. Eighty. The headlights of the car behind flashed on, and he could not tell whether it was catching up on him or not. He did not think it likely.

A fox darted across the road.

"God!" cried Dimmock.

He jammed on his brakes but couldn't miss it. He felt the thud, felt the wheel quiver, and for a moment almost lost control. Ugh! He shuddered, but regained control as the near side wing passed within an inch of a tree trunk. "Nearly had it," he said fiercely. "I'll show the swine." But he was more wary, not sure what might leap out of the darkness.

He reached the end of the long, straight stretch, and although he could see the glow of headlights in the distance, they seemed a comforting way behind. He was

41

only five miles from Lauriston, and no one knew this section of the road better than he. The only danger would be from a cyclist whose lights didn't show very far, but there wasn't much likelihood of cyclists being on the road as late as this. He swung the wheel right and left, leaning over as if he were on a motorcycle. There was a set grin on his face: he hadn't had a drive like this for forty years, and even then he had been told he was crazy! He scraped the hedges, the tires screamed, the car body quivered and rattled; but soon he saw the pale blue lights of the Wide World Foods plant, which often worked a night shift. The huge plant, which included a cannery, deep freeze, processing and storage plants, covered several square miles. It was about a mile south of the town, with the main London railway on one side, easy for sidings.

Once beyond it he could feel safe. Dimmock slowed down a little. There was no reflection of headlights in the mirror, but that meant nothing because the driver of the other car might have switched down to parking lights on. At forty miles an hour Dimmock drove through the silent town, and then saw two men at a corner: policemen.

He jammed on his brakes and slithered to a stop.

A constable and a sergeant came towards him, and as he leaned out the sergeant said:

"Going a bit fast, sir, aren't you? Who—oh, it's Dr Dimmock." His disapproval eased only slightly.

"Hallo, sergeant," Dimmock said jerkily. "Believe it or not, I've just avoided a hold-up in the forest. Three men in a big black car. Fired at me. Look at the bullet hole in the back if you don't believe me."

Disapproval vanished.

"*Fired* at you, sir?"

Five times. If that car comes along here, stop it. Be careful, though. Who's on duty at the police station tonight?"

"Superintendent Farley's in charge, sir."

"I'm going to see him," Dimmock said, and could not conceal the fact that he was as excited as a schoolboy. "Murderous brutes. Be careful." He let in the clutch and shot off again, leaving two policemen who did not know whether to believe him or not.

"I didn't smell any drink," the sergeant said thoughtfully. "I—hey, look, Bob."

A car came swinging round the corner of the High Street, moving quite as fast as the doctor's car. It was big and dark. Only the sidelights were on, and no more were needed here in the well-lit High Street. The sergeant and the constable moved as one, and it did not seem to occur to either of them to fear that the men in the car were armed.

"Nip across and watch the other side," the sergeant said. "When they see we mean business they'll probably make a dash for it." He saw the constable run across the road, twenty yards in front of the approaching car, and he himself waved it down.

It didn't slacken speed at all. He realized at the last moment that he was within an ace of being run over. He backed desperately, felt the wind of the car, stumbled and fell backwards, and his helmet bumped on the ground like cardboard.

The car disappeared round a corner.

The sergeant scrambled to his feet, but swayed, and when he tried to speak, his speech was slurred. The constable came hurrying.

"You all right, Fred? Fred——"

"All ri'," grunted the sergeant. "They're after Dimmock. Get my bike. Get a call out. Car without a number-plate."

The constable raced across the road, leapt on a bicycle which was standing against the wall of a house, and cycled as if his life depended on it. The sergeant followed a little unsteadily, and listened for the sound of shooting, now sure that Dr Dimmock hadn't been suffering from D.T.s.

He heard the sound of the car engine fade, but no shooting.

The constable saw the racing car swing towards Bournemouth and the coast, then saw Dr Dimmock's car parked outside the police station, where two policemen were standing on duty and a blue light showed. Men weren't usually on guard like this; Dimmock had probably arranged it with the Super.

Dimmock, eyes blazing, face vivid in his excitement, grey hair standing on end, was striding about the Superintendent's office, banging a clenched fist into the palm of his other hand, telling the whole story with graphic emphasis. Superintendent Farley knew him well as a police surgeon, and also knew how lively he could get in his cups, but this wasn't a question of alcoholic exuberance.

While Dimmock was spluttering, Farley lifted a telephone and said quietly:

"We want a car stopped, and a description radioed round at once, Inspector. Ready . . ." he waved Dimmock to a frenzied silence. "A big saloon car, probably black, number not known, looked about fifteen years old, square back . . . Three men believed to be in it . . . Passed through the town within the last few minutes, and could have been heading for Bournemouth or the west . . . Yes, get the call out right away." He rang off and stood up, a tall, darkish, slow-speaking man. "They'll get it, Arthur," he said soothingly.

"What the hell's the matter with you?" demanded Dimmock. "Told you they were armed, didn't I? Why didn't you warn your chaps?"

"If you're sure they were armed, I'll send a supplementary message, but I don't want to raise an alarm if there's any doubt."

"Why, you disbelieving son of Thomas, I told you they fired at me! Warn your chaps before they get shot to ribbons, then give me a drink." Unexpectedly, Dimmock dropped into an armchair and mopped his forehead. In a few seconds he changed from an excited, fiery, powerful-looking man to one who seemed old and tired and pale. "Not so young as I used to be," he said. "Can't stand the excitement. Thing that worries me is, does this explain what happened to Korven?"

"What's this about Korven?" asked Farley sharply.

"Oh, I know, you never approved of me taking him on, but he's a damned good doctor," Dimmock said, "and I'm worried about him."

Before he could go on, a message came from the sergeant who had seen Dimmock outside. Immediately Farley sent out the warning about armed men. Then he listened intently to Dimmock's story, made notes, and sent out a call for Korven and the Vespa. It was nearly half-past two. Now very tired and suffering from reaction, Dimmock didn't argue when Farley said he would drive him home and have a constable deliver the car later.

"Coming in for a quick one?" Dimmock asked outside his house, without any enthusiasm at all.

"Not tonight, Arthur, thanks. Think you can find the keyhole?"

"I'll find the keyhole a lot quicker than you'll find those murderous crooks," Dimmock said gruffly. "Thanks for the lift. Ask your chap to park the car outside the garage, it won't do any harm tonight. 'Night."

"Good night."

Dimmock went quite briskly up to the front door of his house, and Farley drove off, hoping that the old boy didn't get any early calls. Farley, who seldom had to deal with deeds of violence, was wondering what action he ought to take next.

Dimmock opened the front door at the first attempt. He was tired, that was all, he always felt a bit giddy when tired. He hadn't had enough liquor to make a kitten drunk. What he wanted was a cup of coffee and a sandwich: he was one of the rare birds who slept better after coffee. Mabel might have left a snack for him, she often did if she thought he was coming in late.

He stepped towards the kitchen.

The door of the room on the right was open. He noticed that and the darkness beyond, but did not notice the man standing there. He passed this door and was in the kitchen doorway when he heard a rustle of sound behind him.

"That you, Mabel?" he asked, and turned slowly and almost irritably.

He saw a man, a small man, with a knife in his raised right hand.

Dimmock did not even cry out as the knife stabbed into his chest.

5. Inquest

"SOME of the aspects of this deplorable, this heartbreaking affair cannot yet be seen clearly," the coroner said at the postponed inquest on Dr Arthur Dimmock, "but certain facts have now been established, as you have heard from the testimony of the police. It is not my duty as coroner, or your duty as a coroner's jury, to try to give guidance as to the part played by the men in the automobile who it appears attempted to hold Dr Dimmock up in Conne Forest. It is not even our duty to attempt to discover motives. Still less is it our duty to comment upon the circumstances which led to Dr Dimmock's decision to employ as an assistant a young general practitioner with so little experience and with such a—ahem—different background.

"Our duty is to look at the facts as presented to us, and to decide upon our verdict.

"I have no desire to influence the members of the jury unduly, but I would be doing less than my duty if I were not to remind them of certain established facts, to wit:

"On the night in question Dr Korven visited a patient, one Mrs Hill, who had been struck down by paralysis and who, unfortunately, has not yet recovered her power of speech. Dr Korven left, promising to return at ten o'clock. He failed to return. He failed to report to Dr Dimmock. It is established that three small boys cycling near the cottage were impudent to him, a fact which is no doubt deplorable. It is further established that he drove through the village of Conne towards the forest. He was not seen alive again.

"However, at Dr Dimmock's home, and near the body after the cruel murder, one of Dr Korven's gloves was found. Several small jet black hairs were found near the body, and we have heard evidence that such hairs might easily fall out of a man's head when he was rubbing or, ah, scratching."

The coroner, a man of forty with the manner of one of seventy, paused to allow that statement to register on the members of the jury, which included one woman. Then he went on quietly and almost as impressively as he meant to make it:

"We have also established that the killer's knife, found in the garden of Dr Dimmock's house, was one which belonged to Dr Korven. That is beyond all doubt.

"There is the unexplained matter of the car which followed Dr Dimmock through the Forest of Conne, and the men who Dr Dimmock said fired at him. You have also heard evidence that bullet marks were found in the back of the car and others on the forest road. We have another sad fact to acknowledge, that Dr Korven's body was found in the sea near Tingish Head, and that the wreckage of his motor-driven machine was found near the same place. It would not be surprising, therefore, if it were to be established that Dr Korven was in

47

the house when Dr Dimmock returned. However, there appears to be no good reason why Dr Korven should wish to kill a man who was, after all, his benefactor.

"If you agree, members of the jury, that I have given you a fair outline of the circumstances as we know them, then I feel sure that you will bring in a verdict consonant with the opinion that Dr Dimmock was murdered by some person or persons unknown."

Larry Hill, who had been at the back of the schoolroom where the inquest had been held, was among the first to leave. He looked ten years older than he had when Korven had visited him, and harassed and worried. At home, Jane was up and about, but still sick and unable to throw off the effects of the seizure. She had not been able to utter a word since the stroke, and although for a few days she had seemed better both mentally and physically, now she was worse.

She was a ghost of the girl he had loved so much.

In ten days the cottage had lost its sparkle. The little work Jane did was half-hearted and lackadaisical. Her eyes were dull. The doctors, including a London specialist who had since examined her, could find no reason for any of this, and if she did not show a marked improvement within the next week she was to go into the hospital for observation.

Larry's sister was making heavy weather of looking after young James and the cottage.

Larry stepped into the bright sunlight of Lauriston High Street. There was no one here whom he wanted to talk to, and he ought to hurry back to his work at Wide World Foods, but he couldn't concentrate, couldn't free his mind from a fact which no one else seemed to have noticed.

Both doctors had died after seeing Jane.

It couldn't be more than coincidence: but it would not let him alone.

He took his bicycle from a parking place and cycled towards the Wide World Foods plant. He had a double job: storekeeper much of the time and emergency delivery van driver in the rest, taking supplies of various canned processed and deep frozen foods to shops and wholesalers in the Lauriston and Winchester districts.

It was a little after twelve o'clock when he arrived, fifty minutes to lunchtime. He had brought sandwiches and meant to work through his lunch hour; he'd had far too much time off lately, and it wouldn't help if he lost his job.

Mr Pettigrew, the Despatch Department manager, was sitting in his little office when Larry entered. Larry clocked in and went to get the documents he would need; records of goods which had been delivered and others which had been taken out of the different warehouses, where great stocks of foods were stored. He heard Pettigrew coming after him, on his little, sharp-sounding shoes. He did not like Pettigrew and knew that the manager had no liking for him; but they had mutual respect, for no other men had the same exhaustive knowledge of the stocks in the warehouse. Pettigrew was a little round-faced balding man, with a thin voice.

"Oh, Larry." He seldom used the Christian name, and that surprised Larry, who turned quickly.

Pettigrew said: "I have——" and then stopped and gulped. He didn't want to say what was in his mind, which meant that it was something unpleasant. Was it possible that Pettigrew had seized upon the fact of his recent time off to persuade the management to give him notice? A new kind of fear took hold of Larry.

"Yes, what is it?" he asked curtly.

Pettigrew moistened his lips. He certainly didn't relish what he had to say, and if he started offering hypocritical condolences, that would be the last straw.

"Larry," Pettigrew said stiffly. "Have you had a message?"

"No, what kind of message?"

"I'm sorry," Pettigrew said. "I sent it through to the main office, I hoped they—I'm sorry. It's from your sister. You must get home quickly. Your wife has taken a turn for the worse." He stood stiffly, as at attention, and it was easy to see the compassion in the eyes behind those rimless glasses. "Take as much time as you need, Larry. Your job will be quite safe, I have the management's assurance on that. And you may take a van."

Jane died that evening; it was as if she had lost the will to live.

BOOK II

THE VILLAGE OF SILENCE

6. A Report For Dr Palfrey

ON THE day after Jane Hill died, Dr Stanislaus Alexander Palfrey sat at his large desk in his large, underground, airconditioned office, and read the inquest reports in *The Times* and the *Daily Globe*. The *Daily Globe* carried pictures of the two doctors, as well as headlines about the inquest story. There was a photograph of Korven, in a rather thoughtful and pensive mood, and Palfrey studied this, his lips set a little tightly, as if what he was thinking was unpleasant. After a few minutes he put the newspapers down, and stood up and went to a steel filing cabinet in a corner. The cabinet could only be opened with the proper key. Anyone who tried to force it would succeed only in destroying the documents inside, for a self-igniting system was controlled, like so many things here, by electric impulses. Palfrey, a tall, lean man with a slight stoop, wearing a formal black coat and striped trousers, took out a manilla folder from a section marked K. He locked the cabinet again and took the folder to the desk. When he opened it, a much larger photograph of Dr Korven lay in front of him.

"All over, Abe," he said, a kind of valediction. "I couldn't be more sorry." He glanced through the details on the papers in the file, details which showed that Wilberforce Abraham Korven's past had been investigated with infinite thoroughness before he had been accepted as a member of Z5. There were five hundred such members, men and women, of all races, colours, nationalities and religions, a complete cross-section of the people of the world. East and West were represented; nationals of nations hostile to each other often worked

53

together for Z5, which had first claim on their loyalty.

Palfrey knew each agent.

What was in some ways as important, each one knew and accepted his leadership, absolutely.

Korven had.

The Russian, Stefan Andromovitch, had for many years: and the American Cornelius Bruton, and many others.

Israelis and Egyptians, Spaniards and Russians, Chinese and Japanese, French and Arab, all had representatives among the five hundred and two. Every nation contributed to the costs, even Russia, after a lapse of several years. It was simple fact that an agent would lay down his life for that obscure, little-known, often derided organization. Some years earlier, at the time of the great flood caused by the *octi* which had almost swamped the civilized world, an American journal with a vast circulation had published a story on Z5, and in many respects it had been very close to the truth.

The salient points were these:

This world-wide organization, with its headquarters in England, had started during the second World War as an Allied Secret Service, and discovered soon after the war that private individuals were striving to take advantage of the prevailing conditions to make great fortunes or to obtain great power. So Z5 had been commissioned to work against them, and over the years it had become truly international. Where nations quarrelled or fought, Z5 took no active part. Where the hyenas came to feed off the economic flesh of the victims of war, Z5 laboured hard. If one power supplied arms to another, that was outside the scope of Z5. If one particular great combine of arms manufacturers supplied those arms, then it was Z5's affair.

At first, few governments had taken it seriously.

Today, all governments knew that it was a vital link between the world of yesterday and of tomorrow.

Here was an age when power could be gathered into the hands of a few; when one or two men could conceivably control some new scientific secret which could cause death and disaster, or else bring economic ruin to the world. So Z5 was a kind of international secret service, forever on the lookout for people or things which might menace nations, or goodwill, or the future.

Palfrey was its leader responsible to none but himself. And Wilberforce Abraham Korven had become a member only six months earlier. He had been born in Kenya, and as a youth, shown great gallantry against Mau-Mau. As reward, he had been brought to England to complete his medical training.

Palfrey had great need of doctors.

He marked the file and put it into another drawer, where there were records of many dead, then went back to his desk. He did not sit down. He did not like this underground room, and much preferred one from which he could look out of the window into the street and see a little of the passing pageant. Here he felt stifled; yet his fellow agents had decreed that he was too precious for normal risks, insisted that his office should be impregnable, his records inaccessible except to Z5 members. There was so much to do that he spent a great deal of time here. It was easy to forget that he was married, that he had a twelve-year-old son, that he had once lived a free-and-easy social life. There were times when the restrictions imposed by the task were so repressive that he felt he would have to give it up, that someone else must take over, as he had once taken over from the Marquess of Brett.

Then something like the death of Korven made him forget everything but the work.

He lifted a telephone, and a man answered.

"Hallo, Jim. Is Stefan in?"

"Yes, he's just finished a call to Beirut."

"Put me through to him, will you?" As Palfrey waited,

his hand strayed to his thin, silky, golden hair and he began to twist a few strands round his forefinger, a habit which he had tried unsuccessfully to check over the years. He looked rather tired and perhaps a little weak; at first glimpse it was easy to believe that he had a stoop, a receding chin and a vacuous expression. He would have given that impression just then, but when another man spoke to him his whole mood and expression changed. Strength came into his face, a glint in his eyes, firmness in his voice.

"Hallo, Stefan. Can you spare ten minutes?"

"At once, Sap."

"Fine," said Palfrey and rang off, smiled, then patted the strands of hair back into place, incidentally making an absurd little kiss curl, and pulled a note pad towards him. He wrote down half a dozen names, then lifted the receiver again.

"Jim?"

"Yes."

"Call Budapest, Pau, Cairo, Buenos Aires, New York and Aden, will you, and ask for reports on Case 37. I'd like 'em quickly."

"I'll fix it," promised the man named Jim.

"Thanks." Palfrey put down the receiver as the door opened. It was a door of rather more than average height, but the man who came in had to duck very low to avoid banging his head. He was not only tall but massive, a positive giant. Few people really believed in him when they saw him for the first time; it was like looking at an hallucination. His hair had once been dark but was now nearly snow white, giving a distinction which went well with his size. He was good-looking, despite his large features, but it was less his looks than his expression which was impressive, once one got over the shock of his hugeness.

He looked contented; a good man, with something of the calm expression of a priest or an escetic.

He closed the door quietly.

"Hallo, Sap," he said, "I expected to hear from you." He glanced at the newspapers on the big desk. "How are you?"

"I think I'm very worried," Palfrey said mildly.

"I have yet to know the time when you weren't. About Korven?"

"Partly. We haven't had a single report from any agent on Case 37, and that's remarkable."

"How long had it been under review?" the giant asked. He dropped into an armchair made specially for him and stretched out fantastically long legs. His English was excellent, if at times a trifle pedantic; few would have suspected that he was a Russian. But Stefan Andromovitch was now Number 2 in Z5. "Three months?"

"Eleven weeks," said Palfrey. "I've just sent round for reports."

"Yes," said Andromovitch, "you had to do that. Not a single report of any kind yet, you say?"

"All completely negative," Palfrey told him, and began to play with his hair again. "All we know is that Rondivallo disappeared thirteen weeks ago, and that one of his lights o' love died after a throat infection which made her dumb and temporarily paralysed. There were some signs of œdema of the glottis, but that wasn't the cause of death. We've had a man trying to trace Rondivallo's movements in every place he'd visited in the previous twelve months and they might have been following a will-o'-the-wisp. And now Korven, who was trying to find out what Rondivallo did in the Forest of Conne, goes like this after seeing a woman who died from causes which were very like those of Rondivallo's girl friend. I've seen the post-mortem report: it doesn't help. We can't trace the cause, the infection or anything."

"Sure there's nothing else to find at Conne?"

"Not on the surface, anyhow. I talked to the Yard last night. They've checked closely with the Lauriston police. Mitchison did the post-mortem on Mrs Hill. It showed nothing except these vague signs of œdema of the glottis and signs of acute anæmia. All we've got to work on are the unknown people who attacked Dimmock, and the fact that Korven was last seen in Conne village. He wasn't noticed on the other side of the forest, but almost certainly would have been if he'd driven through. We've had a close check made but can't find any witness. Notice anything that it would be easy to miss about the whole thing?"

Andromovitch said promptly:

"Both dead doctors went to see the woman, Jane Hill, within a few hours of the seizure."

"That's it."

"There is another angle," Andromovitch said.

"Tell me."

"Did this Jane Hill, did her husband, did Dimmock, know Rondivallo?"

"Ah," said Palfrey and alertness leapt back into his eyes. "Couldn't see the wood for the trees. Yes. Well, we want someone down at Conne quickly. Any idea who?"

"Matt Stone," Andromovitch answered.

"American, and an enthusiastic English countryside lover, yes. We'll have him here this afternoon and go over everything with him," Palfrey declared. "We'll have time to prepare a briefing." He lifted his telephone. "Jim, have Matthew Stone here at half-past two, will you? . . . Yes, through the shop . . . Thanks."

He rang off as Andromovitch stood up; Palfrey had to crane his neck to look at him.

"I'm still trying to find out who's breaking the oil pipeline in Jacca," the Russian said. "Aly Senaddi is coming to see me at half-past eleven. I'll let you know if there is anything useful to report."

"Fine," Palfrey said, almost absently.

When the door closed he sat quite still for a long

time. The rather vacuous expression was on his face again; a few strands of the silken, golden hair stood out from his forehead. He stayed absolutely still until he jumped up and went to the filing cabinets. This time he took a file out of the bulkier S section—*Stone, Matthew Charles*, and carried it back to his desk. A full-face photograph showed an eager-eyed, youthful-looking man, probably in the early thirties. Profile, he proved to have a snub nose and a stronger chin than most, and very small ears; there was a merry look about him. He had short fair hair, which one photograph showed in a crew-cut.

Palfrey studied the typewritten details.

> Born: 1925, at Phoenix, Arizona, U.S.A.
> Journalist. Education: Phoenix High,
> Arizona University, special subjects
> English Literature, British History,
> North American history. Specialist
> abilities: Judo, ju-jitzu, boxing, cow-
> punching, fencing, ballistics, flying.
> Singe.

There were other details, including the years Stone had spent in the armed forces, mostly in the United States Air Force, a period of post-graduate study in Paris, Rome and London, the fact that he had settled at least temporarily in London. He had been brought into the service of Z5 at a time of urgent investigations into the activities of a so-called oil-drilling company in Arizona. As far as it was known, no one outside this building knew that he was a member of the department.

He had the patience needed, as well as the ability to act swiftly. He would have to be told everything about the mysterious dumbness followed by anæmia and death, and told of all that had happened to Korven.

Palfrey spent the next hour deliberating, but all the time there was one question at the back of his mind:

what had happened to Korven, and what had he discovered? Would he have been killed if he hadn't made some vital discovery?

The telephone bell rang. Palfrey moved his hand towards it, hesitated, lifted it when it rang again, and said in a husky voice:

"Yes, Jim?"

He listened for a moment, and the metamorphosis came again. The hint of weakness and the suggestion of languor vanished, he looked younger, the expression in his eyes became alert and commanding.

"All right, Jim," he said. "I'll get in touch with Budapest myself. Get me through." He put the receiver down and flicked on an inter-office talking machine. "Stefan," he said, "get the job you're on parcelled up and handed over to someone else. We'd better both work on Case 37. There's a report in from Budapest, but not direct from Cornell himself—from Raison who had to contact Cornell over another job. Cornell had a stroke yesterday. He was paralysed for twelve hours, but the paralysis seems to have gone, except in his throat. He's lost his voice."

Andromovitch said slowly, softly: "Like the Hill woman."

"That's right," said Palfrey. "I'm going to talk to Raison, and we'd better get Mitchison flown out to Budapest, he's the most likely man—all right, forget it, I'm talking to myself." He flicked the talking machine off and lifted a telephone, almost in the same movement. Give me Farraday, Jim . . . Hallo, Farry, listen. Cornell has had a stroke at his Budapest hotel. I want Mitchison to fly out and find out what's caused it. See if Mitchison can go at once. Then find out from him who is the best man on the spot and arrange for that man to examine Cornell immediately. Fix everything for Mitchison: airplane tickets, hotels. Make it desperately urgent." Palfrey rang off, but lifted the telephone again at once. "Jim," he said. "Yes, I'll hold on." He was staring at the blank wall in front of him, and his eyes were hard, his lips set tightly. "Hallo, Jim, yes. Check all the others on Case 37. Send Gully over to Budapest to take over, he's briefed on the case. Right? . . . Thanks."

He rang off.

He sat absolutely still, staring at the wall where there was nothing to see, until the telephone bell rang, and he was on to Budapest.

But he learned nothing new, except that Cornell was still alive and seemed to be quite well, except for his loss of voice. A doctor had reported symptoms rather like œdema of the glottis, with the swollen, constricted throat. He was taking swabs and specimens of saliva, which should help Mitchison later

That was at twelve-fifteen.

At a quarter to one a report came in from New York; the Z5 man who had been checking Rondivallo's movements there had just been stricken by paralysis.

At two-fifteen, swiftly upon each other, came the news that the agent in Cairo and the one in Pau had been stricken in exactly the same way.

"Now we've got to have each man examined at once, and each man's movements checked. We've got to find out what they knew, how far they'd got," Palfrey said in a tense voice. "Five of them, and the only two who still seem all right are Brown in Buenos Aires and Miller in Aden."

At two-twenty-nine Matthew Stone came into the office. As he was approaching Palfrey's desk a telephone bell rang. Palfrey picked it up, said "Sorry" abruptly to the young American and then into the telephone: "Yes, Jim?" He set his jaw as he listened and Andromovitch, who had been waiting there with him to talk to Stone, saw exactly how this latest news hurt.

Palfrey said: "That makes it a nap hand," and rang

off. He sat still, pale, obviously on edge. He gave a slight nod to Andromovitch and added abruptly: "Brown's down with it, too." He looked broodingly at Stone, who returned his gaze quite calmly.

"All right Matt, come and sit down," Palfrey said at last. "I don't know what's going on, but I know we're in for a hell of a time. The first thing I want to do is remind you that if you'd rather back out, now's the chance. This could be much deadlier than the Arizona job.

7.   Matt Stone

MATTHEW STONE thought: "I've never seen him looking like this," as he advanced towards Palfrey, then waited until Palfrey had finished with the telephone.

He had known Palfrey for over four years, and had accepted him without question as one of the world's great men. He could never define or describe it, but he had felt the influence of Palfrey from their first meeting. Palfrey had a kind of natural authority and the gift of being able to command loyalty. Perhaps it was due mostly to his single-mindedness: nothing ever appeared to make him deviate from a chosen course.

Palfrey looked his age: forty-one or two.

He also looked angry; coldly angry. When he offered Matt the opportunity to withdraw from the job, he spoke with a kind of savage intentness which told a story of its own.

Matt said quietly: "I don't want to withdraw, Sap. Ever since I had your message I've been looking forward to hearing all about the job." He had something of the drawl of the far West in his voice; his crewcut, his bow tie, the cut of his silk suit of a pale biscuit colour, all marked him as an American. He had pale grey eyes, which hadn't shown like that in the photographs. "So why don't you go ahead and tell me?"

"Pull up a chair," Palfrey said, and Åndromovitch did so for Matt, who said "Thanks" and dropped into it. Andromovitch leaned back in the larger chair, as if this were a pleasant afternoon session. There was no hint of tension about him, and it was the absence of tension in Stone which made him an unusual agent. Palfrey had never seen him anything but completely relaxed.

"Do you mind if I smoke?"

"Carry on," said Palfrey. "I've been trying to cut the damned things down." He pushed a box across the desk, and an ashtray after it. "Heard of Rondivallo?" he asked, out of the blue.

Matt didn't blink.

"Sure," he said, and into his mind there flashed a recollection of all that he had ever heard of Rondivallo; but he waited for Palfrey to speak again.

"What do you know about him?" Palfrey asked.

"One of the lesser known physicists," Matthew said. "Maybe he wouldn't have been known at all if it wasn't for his name. If you want to know what's in a name, think of Rondivallo. He's Australian. He first came into prominence with a paper on the effects of radio-activity on animal life in the Australian outback, and he made that his special study. His purpose, according to all he said himself, and he was a loudmouth, was to find means of curing illness caused by exposure to radio-active dust. He spent some time in Japan, working in the hospitals where some of the victims of the atom bombs in Hiroshima and Nagasaki were still living. As far as I can recall, he was never able to report any positive results, but every now and again he would get his name in the newspapers, over a dame I guess, and he was always asked how his research was progressing. He invariably gave the same answer: he figured he was on the verge of a great discovery. About a year ago he left Australia on a world tour and said he was aiming to consult with others who had been working on the same lines. He turned up in Buenos Aires, New York, Aden and Cairo, some place in Eastern Europe, either Bucharest or Budapest, and some place in France with a short name, I don't recall it at the moment. Every time he had his photograph in the newspapers he had a blonde with him. A different blonde." Matt paused for a moment, then gave a half-hearted kind of grin. "I may be wrong about that. Maybe one of them was a brunette."

All the time he had been leaning back and talking in his quiet voice, with the up-and-down cadence which seemed to be held severely in check. He knew that this would most impress Palfrey and Andromovitch, and it was vitally important to impress them well. But when he stopped talking there was no hint on his face of the anxiety he felt.

Palfrey's lips twitched in a smile.

"Did you tell him who the subject of Case 37 was?" Andromovitch asked dryly.

"No, no one told me," said Matt unhurriedly. "I just happen to have that kind of mind." He saw the Russian's grin, and relaxed. "Okay, I fell for that. How much did I get wrong?"

"You didn't get anything wrong, but there are some things you don't know," said Palfrey. "We sent a man to check on Rondivallo about three months ago, when he was due to arrive in London and didn't turn up. All nuclear scientists are kept under surveillance, just to try to make sure they don't vanish. The Special Branch chaps lost Rondivallo, who was a good all-round research man, not just a glamour boy. We're only now beginning to discover the ramifications of radio-activity on animal life, much of what we read about is guesswork. We do know that it can have deadly results, and we also know that in two cases women have died in circumstances not unlike victims of radio-active poisoning. We don't know any more than that. We do know that it kills. We also know that it could have to do with Rondivallo's activities. Events in Conne make it urgent to find out what's going on."

Palfrey began to play with some strands of hair.

"We're a kind of supra-national group, of course, and don't take sides," he went on. "But now and again we come across something like this which is being developed by a national interest. Whenever we do, we report it to a United Nations Secretariat and forget it. It's possible that this is such a job. But no single nation showed the slightest unwillingness to let us search for Rondivallo, who has globe-trotted pretty widely. We half believed that he'd vanished with one of his lovelies, lying low until his money ran out. But in the past when he's vanished it's only been for three or four weeks. Since he vanished from the Forest Hotel, near Conne, we haven't had a single line on him. If he'd found a love-nest somewhere and was just getting out of the public eye, we would have traced him. But his light o' love down in Hampshire is missing, too—an Irish girl working at the Forest Hotel, where Rondivallo stayed. The hotel is a luxury place and extremely well run."

"May I stay there?" Matt interpolated mildly.

"Yes. No one's had any luck in looking for Rondivallo, remember," Palfrey went on, "but among the places he often visited was the little village of Conne, near the forest of the same name. He spent a lot of time in an agricultural research station in the forest. The place wasn't very elaborate, what we would have expected to interest Rondivallo. The research work was done in a cottage, one of several owned by the hotel proprietors. Rondivallo said that he had to study the results of his major experiments while at Conne. He had no laboratory, or at best a patchwork one. He did have his new lovely, Maureen O'Shea."

Matt said: "A redhead, according to the newspapers,"

then wished he hadn't spoken; these two might soon begin to think that he was a blow-off.

"A redhead," agreed Palfrey mildly. "They left about three months ago, and neither of them has been seen since. That was Rondivallo's last public appearance." He paused and Matt waited, believing that they would soon be at the crux of the matter. "We sent a man down there, a coloured general practitioner named——"

"Korven," Matt intervened, and could have kicked himself. He was so annoyed that he actually sat up, and went on ruefully: "Sometimes I wish I could keep my big mouth shut. I was reading about Korven in this morning's newspapers, and this pigeonhole I've got for a mind worked again."

"I shouldn't try to stop it from working," Palfrey said dryly. "Yes, Korven. He attended a patient who had suffered from a mysterious stroke—the Conne woman named Hill. I'm going to give you a full report on the seizure and death, everything you need to know. For a start: five of our agents are suffering from a similar sickness, according to reports received today."

"I can imagine why you're interested in Rondivallo," Matt said quietly.

He was still sitting bolt upright.

Something in the way Palfrey had told the story, as well as the fact themselves, had got into him. He was desperately anxious to say the right thing.

It came.

"You want me to start in at once, I imagine."

"As soon as you've had time to think about what you'll need," Palfrey said.

"Sure," said Matt. "I'll think about it in the next half hour. Will that be soon enough?"

"He isn't over-confident, is he?" Palfrey asked Andromovitch.

"I think he was a little nervous in case he was creating that impression," the Russian said. "I don't think you will have any cause to complain about the way he goes about this, Sap."

"Well," Matt Stone mused as he sat back in the rest room of the underground offices, still recumbent in an easy chair, "I've been warned, and they didn't pull any punches. I wish I didn't know as much as I do about the symptoms of radio-active dust poisoning."

He lit a cigarette, then stretched out a hand and pressed a bell push. When the door opened and a middle-aged, grey-haired woman entered, he gave his attractive smile and said:

"Do you think you could rustle up some English tea for me?"

"Of course, Mr Stone," the woman said. "I won't be many minutes. Would you like some cakes?"

"Cookies?"

"Shall we settle for French pastries?" She asked that with a smile.

Matt laughed, and was glad that he could laugh freely. But the thought soon faded. He pondered deeply over everything Palfrey had told him and everything he knew; then began to wonder what Palfrey expected him to need for the job.

The woman came in with a laden tray and far too many French pastries. She put the tray down on a table, and Matt noticed how well kept her hands were, how neatly she dressed; when she went out he noticed her slim legs. She wasn't exactly a serving wench. He had not the faintest idea who she was, and knew that he often worked with Palfrey's agents without realizing it; Spider Palfrey, with his web. S. A. Palfrey made Sap. What a misnomer!

Never mind dreaming; what did he need?

"I don't know how many items I've forgotten," he said to Palfrey a little later. "The way I see it, I don't want to take too much with me, but I could do with a girlfriend, and I should imagine it would be better if she was American. Two Americans would seem more natural than one—or am I dreaming that up? If a job like this is too dangerous for a girl, then perhaps I ought to go alone. Whenever I see two men together on this kind of holiday, I wonder what they're up to. Men don't usually holiday in pairs, they only hunt in them." Palfrey nodded, as if in general agreement. Palfrey was being very cagey. "Also I ought to have photographs of Rondivallo, full face and profile both sides, and a description including identifying marks on the body. And I ought to have a photograph of all these girls of his, including the Irish redhead. Also, a photograph of anyone known to have worked with Rondivallo in England. Any close research associate, for instance, anyone he might know. What do you say for it? The whole works."

"We can arrange all these," Palfrey said, nodding again.

"That's swell. And I ought to have a quick refresher about the district of the Forest of Conne. Also, a refresher about the effects of radio-active dust, any means of identifying it on inanimate as well as animate objects. And I ought to have a suit of chain mail," Matt added. He grinned, then wished he hadn't been facetious; but Palfrey seemed mildly amused. "I ought to know all I can about the Conne woman who died, where she'd been before the seizure, her neighbours, her husband. I ought to have access to the police files on the case, and get all the details I can about the car which followed Dr Dimmock. And I ought to have a radio transmitter, the small kind you showed me three weeks ago, in case I want to get news through in a rush."

Palfrey said: "It'll all be ready by morning, Matt. We'll arrange for you to spend a couple of hours with a

68

research man who can tell you all you want to know. You'd better drive that Chrysler of yours, with the New York number plate. Then you'll look like a genuine tourist."

Matt stood up.

"I am a genuine tourist! Thanks. Sap . . ."

"Yes?"

"Who do I have for company?"

"I think you'll have a girl," Palfrey said. "She's spoiling for work because——" he hesitated, and then added almost abruptly: "Her brother was killed in our last big job. She won't be back to normal until she's really worked herself to a standstill."

Matt didn't speak and didn't move away, but raised one eyebrow slightly as he looked at Palfrey. He was aware of the giant Russian looking at him from the armchair, and could not guess what either was thinking. Then Palfrey said dryly:

"She'll keep her eye on the ball, and she won't do crazy things because she's out for revenge."

"American?"

"No, English," said Palfrey. "She spent most of her childhood in the Lauriston and Conne districts, and knows them well. She's also spent several years in the United States, and anyone who recognized her down at Conne won't be surprised that she's with an American."

"Sounds just right," Matt said. "Thanks." He rubbed his chin. "When do I meet her?"

"Tomorrow, early," Palfrey answered. "I'll tell her to join you in your car at . . ." he gave precise details, and added: "I'll have her bags sent to your car early in the morning. I don't think either of you is being watched, but I'd like you to be as careful as you can. One other thing."

"Yes?"

"You'll probably dislike her intensely, but she has the best qualifications and a very good mind."

"Suits me," Matt sounded as he felt: mostly satisfied, just a little uneasy. He was going into the face of an unknown danger, but he had done that before. Danger didn't scare him until it was past; then he had time to remember how terrified he had been. He had slight mental reservations about the girl companion, but Palfrey wasn't the man to make an elementary mistake. "Am I to be told about what's happened to the other chaps in various places?"

"From time to time," Palfrey promised.

"Thanks," said Matt.

Andromovitch had said practically nothing during either of the interviews, and Matt was now almost uneasily aware of him. It was as if the Russian was appraising him, assessing his weaknesses and his strengths; and he had an odd feeling that the giant was capable of doing that. About him there was a kind of aura, of goodness, of other worldliness. Crazy. And as crazy that he should be a Russian. Fantastic stories of his prodigious strength had reached Matt, but there were similar rumours about a lot of people.

"Do I get any more briefing?" Matt asked.

"No. There are one or two of our chaps on the job down there, and the one you might need is Peters—you'll get a photograph of him and the others, for recognition's sake. You'll give them the usual sign, fingers of the hand spread out, palm towards them, three times in succession. We've one or two other agents you don't know about, but I'll tell you who they are in emergency. The sign will always be recognised, anyhow."

"Sure," Matt said.

"There's only one job," Palfrey added quietly. "Find out why Korven was killed, why Dimmock was killed, and——"

"Look after the dead woman's husband, Larry Hill, and the Carters," Andromovitch contributed at last. "They may be in equal danger."

"You mean, everyone who saw the woman when she was ill might be in danger?"

"That's it," said Palfrey more briskly, and Andromovitch nodded. "Okay, Matt, I'll be in touch."

A telephone bell rang, and Palfrey picked up the instrument, giving a nod of apology. He said, "Yes, Jim," in a way that he had done thousands of times before, but then seemed to grip the telephone more tightly, and bleakness showed in his eyes. As he listened, a faint sound of Jim's voice came into the big room.

"All right," Palfrey said at last. "Thanks, Jim. No, not now." He rang off, and his right hand strayed to his hair as it so often did when he was under stress, and he said: "Cornell died an hour ago. There's a message from Pau saying that our man there isn't likely to last the day out. Same cause, but it's killed quicker. Swelling of the throat, paralysis, sudden anæmia, wasting and death."

Matt felt the intensity of his gaze and the cool appraising gaze of the Russian. This was a kind of test, hurled at him by the circumstances.

"Sap," he said, "are you sure I ought to have the woman with me? Wouldn't it be better to try to handle this alone?"

Palfrey began to smile.

"No," he said. "I'm going to send you photographs of our agent Yvonne Brown, of Rondivallo, and of all his known girlfriends including Maureen O'Shea. Make sure you'll recognise any original you happen to see."

"Right," said Matt, and grinned. "I hope Rondi's taste was good."

8. Visitors to Conne

MATT STONE waited by the side of his powder blue
Chrysler, parked in one of the smaller London squares,
where American cars usually attracted attention. Most
youths and most men who passed glanced at it; most
girls and women glanced at him as he sat at the wheel.
It was a bright morning, although the sun wasn't yet
hot, and he sat relaxed and at ease at the wheel. He
watched the pavement in front, and kept glancing in the
wing mirror so that he could see who was walking
towards him; he hadn't yet met Yvonne Brown. All he
knew was that she would be wearing a pale yellow
linen dress, that she was a brunette, that her name was
so unexpected. He was not sure how old she was,
but the photographs suggested the early thirties. He
told himself that the manner of their meeting was a
piece of pointless play-acting on Palfrey's part, but Palfrey always had a purpose. This could be another kind
of test, the girl's first job might be to tell Palfrey how
he had reacted.

A girl turned the corner behind him, and the sun
made her yellow dress look very bright. He watched as
she came walking towards him. Nice legs, Nice ankles.
Tall. He couldn't see her face and wasn't sure that it
mattered. As she drew nearer he had a peculiar view of
her. Her feet disappeared in the mirror, he could see her
legs, and also her waist and bosom. Well, Palfrey hadn't
exactly wished a hag or a bag on him. She drew nearer,
walking briskly but without any sign of haste, and the
temptation to look round was overwhelming; but Matt
continued to look into the mirror. This might not be
Yvonne Brown, remember. She was on the outside of a

stream of people closest to him. Now he could only see her waist, but he could hear the sharp tap-tap of her footsteps.

She drew up alongside the car.

He put his head through the open window.

"Why, hallo. Yvonne?"

"Yes," she said.

He looked into her face. It was beautiful, and like the photograph, but lifeless. It was easy to understand why he wasn't expected to like her. He didn't like the way she said "yes" or the coldness of her expression or the aloofness of her manner. She was English "county" at its stuffiest. All these thoughts went through Matt's mind as he slid out of the car and held the door open for her.

"Won't you get in?"

"Thank you." Words could be made of ice, and these were very close to it. He shut the door on her and went round to the other side, to get in. At least fifty people were in the square, but for a few moments Matt hardly noticed any of them. He felt mad at Yvonne Brown. Then he glanced into the wing and driving mirrors again, to see if anyone was showing interest in her or in him. No one appeared to be. He started the engine, waited for an errand boy to pass, and then slid forward. By then, he had decided to behave as if this woman was the friendliest, fluffiest little creature imaginable, as warm as she was frigid. It was no use nursing himself into a mood of resentment because Palfrey had wished an iceberg onto him.

He gave her his brightest smile.

"Did they make a mystery of me to you too?"

"Mystery?" She wasn't even going to co-operate.

"Did they show you a photograph?"

"Yes," she answered, and did not trouble to ask if he had seen a photograph of her, or to make any comment at all. She sat rather primly. In the wide front seat there was room for another person between them, and Iceberg Yvonne Brown obviously meant to keep at a distance. She wore shoes of soft green leather, and there was no doubt that her legs and ankles were better than most. Her dress was embroidered with small flowers of a slightly paler yellow than the linen itself.

Matt tried again.

"Sap tells me you know the Forest of Conne well."

"Very well."

"Been there recently?"

"No."

Matt looked at the traffic, which was thickening as they neared Piccadilly.

"How about telling me what Sap's told you."

"Very well," she said.

He could have slapped her down, she was so snooty; but he accepted the situation now. He manœuvred the big car into Piccadilly traffic, taking advantage of every chance he had to forge ahead. At Hyde Park Corner there was a thick knot of traffic which seemed to separate in front of him, and he grinned as he swung round by the hospital, and said:

"That Gordian knot's untied."

She said: "Dr Palfrey told me that . . ."

She had a pleasant voice once she forgot that she was Lady Goddess Almighty, but it wasn't her voice which impressed Matt, it was the way she told her story. This girl had a mind as lucid as infra-red rays. She told everything in detail, which proved conclusively that Palfrey had kept nothing back from her. Yet she did not glance at Matt as he drove at nearer forty than thirty.

". . . and of course we have to try to find out what caused Mrs Hill's seizure, and the essential thing is to trace her movement on the day she was taken ill; and on the preceding days if necessary."

"That's right," Matt said. "And we have to talk to everyone who saw her after she was struck down, and anyone the doctors might have talked to. Also"—he smiled faintly, and shot her a sidelong glance—"we have to do all this without allowing anyone to suspect that we're interested in her."

"If the task was easy, it would hardly be worth Dr Palfrey's while sending two of us," she said.

Matt looked as if he were startled.

"That's exactly right!" he declared. "How come I didn't think of it? But sarcasm was wasted on her; so was the grin which accompanied it, for she was staring straight ahead.

Matt settled down more comfortably in his seat once they were on the Great West Road, and he felt that he could let the engine all out. Factories, houses, garages, churches and pubs all fell behind; then they hummed past the London Airport; then into Staines.

"You want to stop for coffee?" Matt asked.

"I would rather get on with the job."

"Suits me, but we have to eat."

"We should reach the forest before one o'clock," Yvonne Brown said, "and before we try anywhere else I think we ought to try to get accommodation at the Forest Hotel. It's the obvious place for tourists of our standing. In any case we can get luncheon there."

Matt couldn't resist saying:

"It's where Rondivallo stayed before he vanished, remember."

"Yes, of course."

They drove through Staines.

"Now let's see how soon we can get to the forest." Matt said, and let the great car have its head. It held the road as if it was still, not touching ninety miles an hour. Speed soothed him. "Sap give you photographs of Rondi's girl friends to study?"

"Yes."

"The one he was making hay with down here was quite a picture," Matt observed. "An Irish redhead."

"She was bright chestnut," declared Yvonne Brown.

"Okay," Matt said, and sighed. "Light bright chestnut."

The Forest Hotel stood in its own grounds on the Winchester side of the forest. It was on a hill, and had views over the forest and the rolling countryside beyond. Bordering the forest were the great market gardens and orchards which helped to feed the Wide World Foods plant, and beyond the fields was the English Channel. They could just see the sea as they got out of the car in front of the huge doors and the wide stone steps of the hotel. It looked more like a private house, with its arched, mullioned window, its iron work, its pale grey stone.

"Someone's ancestral home," Matt observed, and looked up at a great coat-of-arms emblazoned on the stained-glass window atop the front door.

"Yes," Yvonne said.

He had an odd feeling, when they went inside, that they were expected or at least were recognised. He was used to the friendliness and often the courtesy of the English, but they seemed to be a little over-obsequious here; perhaps Yvonne had that effect on them. A faded, greying man at the desk in the hall, which looked like the hall of a miniature castle, greeted them.

Yes, there were rooms, each with a bathroom.

Yes, they were in good time for luncheon.

Yes . . .

They went straight to the dining-room, which was large, and panelled in baronial hall style; six waitresses were all easy on the eye.

Theirs was a girl with more than her share of looks and with light auburn hair. She wasn't the missing Maureen O'Shea, but was very like her, and her Irish brogue was as lilting as a brogue could be.

Yvonne did not seem to notice this.

Service and food were so good that it was almost suspicious. Had Palfrey laid it on? Once before he, Matt, had gone to a hotel and found that it had been filled with Z5 members. This one, too? He didn't really think so. He noticed with wry amusement that Yvonne seemed as hungry as he was.

He pushed his plate aside.

"For a soufflé, that had most of my Paris friends beaten," he said. "Where do you suggest we go first?" He had decided that the Irish girl could be tackled later.

"You are in charge," Yvonne said, and glanced round quickly, as if to make sure that they hadn't been overheard. No one was near them.

"I'd like to look over the terrain," Matt agreed, "and also the place where Rondivallo worked. We need to see the cottage where Mrs Hill collapsed, too, and the other where the Carter family lives. Then I'd like to talk to the man Hill, when I can find an excuse."

"I can find one," Yvonne said.

Goddam her, Matt thought; yet in a way she more amused than irritated him.

"Is there a good reason for a tourist to go in that general direction?"

"Oh, yes," Yvonne said. "One of the more interesting Roman burial mounds in the district is near there. Two years ago urns were dug up, and more bones were discovered. It is certainly a place which an American tourist should visit."

She did not even smile.

"According to my memory," Matt said, "this Carter family consists of husband, wife and three children, two of them in the late teens, one about nine. The woman is sour and a gossip, the man a dullard with green fingers. They make a fair living growing vegetables. What do you call that kind of farmer?"

"He is a market gardener."

"Sure, I knew there was a word for it. He lives in a cottage near the hills. Shall we go near there for a start?"

"We can drive on the top road and look down on the cottages about a mile and a half away," Yvonne Brown explained. "From there you can see over the whole of the terrain."

Still she did not smile, but the way she said that made him wonder whether a dry sense of humour was hiding beneath the ice. He was more preoccupied with Yvonne than he wanted to be; the meal had been good enough to make him sleepy.

As he drove away from Forest Hotel, with its well-trained servants and its atmosphere of bygone days, the whole of the Forest of Conne spread out in front of him, and beyond there were the undulating hills of Hampshire, some green, some brown and freshly ploughed, some gold as corn on the great American prairies. There were the big orchards and the neat fields of peas and beans, with dozens of labourers busy in the fields. The sun was hot; it would be easy to doze off.

Matt glanced at Yvonne as they turned out of the gates, soon losing elevation; half of the view had already disappeared. She was staring straight ahead of her, and had quite a profile, Matt already knew: classic was the word.

She told him to take a narrow road to the left. They passed three S bend signs within a mile, and forty miles an hour was the highest safe speed. That suited Matt's mood. Soon they came to a straight stretch of road, rising steep, and Yvonne said:

"If you pull off the road by that oak tree, you can see everything you want to see."

"Fine."

It was quite a tree, with low, spreading branches capturing the sun and making the grass beneath it look black with shadow. He turned into the shade. The ground dropped sharply away from the road, and a small, flat valley lay in front of them, brushed with England's pride. Beyond was the azure blue of the sea, like a sparkling stream.

"My, my," Matt said. "It's quite a place."

She didn't comment, just pointed towards the right. "You can just see the church tower of Conne village, and the red roof of the inn." Her arm moved. "There is the road which leads to the cottage where Jane Hill died. It is the tiled one." Not only that, it looked small and snug, and in the front of it there was a tiny patch of bright colour, the flower garden showing clearly, although this was two miles away. "Over there, beyond the cottage, are the Roman mounds, and to the left, where those three small buildings are grouped, is the Carters' cottage. You can see his smallholding quite well."

"Yes," Matt said. The smallholding land was clearly visible and they could see the straight lines of the growing plants. "You certainly know your terrain," he added dryly.

For the first time she looked at him as if she was going to smile.

They got out of the Chrysler.

A mosquito settled on Yvonne's forehead. With nine people out of ten, Matt would have acted first and laughed afterwards; he would have knocked it off. With her, he said:

"There's a skeeter on your forehead."

"Oh," she said, and shook her head and put her hand up to brush it off. She made a little grimace. "I felt it bite," she added. "Look. Ugh!" She squashed the thing, and it stained a tiny part of her forehead and a tiny part of her finger red with her blood.

They forgot the mosquito.

Coming from the Forest of Conne and the village on the outskirts was a small car. Matt took out a pair of field-glasses and looked through them. The small Austin seemed to keep towards him, and he could see the man and woman sitting in it. The Carters had that model car. They were travelling at quite a speed and were close to the Hills' cottage. They drew level with it and passed. The Carters' home was about a mile and a half away, as far as Matt could judge, and on the road was a little clump of trees. These were probably the Carters.

The small car slowed down, moved off again, and then seemed to sway, as if the driver was out of control.

It started yet again.

Yvonne was watching it intently, while Matt caught a glimpse of a movement among the trees. He did not notice that Yvonne was rubbing at her forehead; he did notice that the driver seemed to be trying to get out of the Austin. At that moment there seemed no significance in either of these things, but when the car stopped he saw two men near the clump of trees, one on either side of the Austin.

The little car's driver was standing by it now, one arm waving, as if pleading for help. Then without a moment of warning, so suddenly that it seemed unreal, there was a flash, a billow of dark smoke hiding the car completely and enshrouding some of the trees.

Yvonne exclaimed.

"What's that?"

"Hold it," Matt said tensely. He saw two men running from the smoke; a moment later they vanished beneath some trees. Now there was a cloud of dark smoke tinged with a red which was getting brighter; the glow of fire. "How fast can we get down to the village?" Matt demanded, and snatched the glasses from his eyes. "We have to cut that pair off."

A car appeared from the shelter of the trees, moving swiftly towards Conne.

"We'll never cut that off," Yvonne said in a thin voice. "They'd be halfway to Lauriston before we reached the village." Her voice was tense and hard. "We might be able to help——"

She broke off.

The smoke was high above the blaze, now, and the fire itself looked like a molten red ball, burning so fiercely that they knew that there wasn't a chance for the two people who had been in the car.

The Carters?

Matt was holding Yvonne's wrist and drawing her towards the Chrysler.

"Get in, and hurry. Can we reach Lauriston before they do?"

"We might be able to, but why?"

He slammed the door and leapt in at the driving seat, and they were moving almost before she had finished the question.

"Which way?" Matt was sharp-voiced.

"The way we came."

Matt swung the car round as if it was a toy, and put his foot down. They seemed to leave the ground as they leapt down the hill. Halfway down, and without taking his gaze off the road, Matt said:

"The Carters had an old Austin. That car was an old Austin. Mrs Carter saw Jane Hill while the doctor was with her. As far as we know, only one other person saw her and talked to the doctors."

"Larry Hill," Yvonne exclaimed.

"Larry Hill."

"When you come to the first crossroads, turn left," she said. "It's a narrow turning but there shouldn't be much traffic and it comes out half a mile this side of the food factory where Hill works."

"Fine," said Matt. "Hold tight."

Out of sight, the old car and the bodies of the Carters burned.

Ten miles away, Larry Hill was checking some packages in the storage bins of the warehouse, forgetful of his grief for a few blessed minutes.

Racing towards Lauriston were the two men in the small car.

It did not matter how desperate the haste, if a road was narrow and winding, real speed was impossible. Tightlipped, Matt put the nose of the Chrysler towards the road on the left, then glanced at Yvonne.

She was rubbing at her forehead.

"Road get any better?" He was fuming.

"Quite straight, a mile or so on."

"We have some luck. That bite irritating?"

"It's not like an ordinary gnat bite, it's stinging," Yvonne said. "More like a wasp sting."

"I've a first-aid kit in the trunk."

"Oh, it's not worth stopping for," Yvonne Brown said.

Then they turned a corner, and the narrow road led straight as Matt could wish for.

He sent the car hurtling along.

9. Snap Decision

"LET's hope to God we're here first," Matt said and slowed down as they approached the big FACTORY ENTRANCE notice on the outskirts of Lauriston. Beyond, he could see a church spire and a few small houses, but the buildings of the Wide World Foods plant were hidden by a high cement wall. No cars were parked outside. Matt peered into his driving mirror, but saw nothing coming along the road behind him, so he pulled into a parking space near the entrance. He jumped out and approached a small gate house. A gatekeeper was sitting looking out of a tiny hatch of a window. Beyond were big yards and many wide roads, and everywhere small delivery vans or huge trucks for long-distance journeys.

"Good afternoon, sir."

"Excuse me," Matt said, as unhurriedly as if this was as casual as asking the way. "Have you seen any cars approach from the direction I came from?" He pointed.

"Can't say I've noticed any, sir, but I couldn't be sure, I've been on the telephone some of the time."

"Thank you. Has any car come in here?"

"Only a van, sir."

"One of your own vans?"

The gatekeeper, spick and span in a navy blue uniform and a peaked hat, hesitated before he replied slowly:

"As a matter of fact, sir, it was Larry Hill's van. But excuse me, may I ask your business?"

Matt beamed.

"Just call me curious," he said. "Do you know if the managing director is in this afternoon?"

The gatekeeper seemed to stiffen.

"Mr Charles Harrison, sir? I understand that he will be in about half past four, sir. If you would care to wait——"

"I might, at that," Matt said. "Thanks a lot, officer. Big place you have here, isn't it?"

"Colossal, sir!" The man's pride was echoed in his voice. "Everything's laid on, too, it's like a town by itself, sir. Got its own playing fields, cinema, gymnasium, hospital, pretty well everything. They look after the employees extremely well."

"Nice thing to hear," Matt said.

He moved away from the gatehouse, as Yvonne opened

83

the door of the Chrysler and put one leg out. It was undoubtedly a very beautiful leg, and it was difficult not to look at it. Then, puzzled because she did not make any further move to get out of the car, he looked at her face. She was bending forward a little, to get out, and holding on to the open door. She seemed stuck.

"You all right?" he asked, and hurried forward.

She drew her leg back.

"I—I'm a bit stiff," she began, and moistened her lips. "I must have been sitting in the wrong position." She managed a kind of smile—at herself, not because she was amused. "I shall be all right." She rubbed at a big reddish splotch on her forehead: the mosquito bite.

"Well, take it easy," Matt said, "and keep away from maneater mosquitoes in future, that one certainly took a liking to you." He spoke almost for the sake of speaking, because she looked pale and there was no longer such calm brightness in her eyes. Was she in pain? One half of his mind was preoccupied with her, the other half with the car which should surely come along the road soon—unless it had already reached this spot and gone past. If it had, then Larry Hill seemed to be in no danger here, for he was safely inside the grounds of the factory. Matt offered cigarettes and she took one. He lit it for her as she settled further back in the car, moving slowly, as if with an effort.

"What are you going to do next?" she asked.

From the beginning, she had articulated with extreme precision; now she seemed to be talking even more slowly and deliberately.

"I'm going to stop the men in that car and hand them over to the police," Matt said, "and I'm going to invoke what Sap always calls Emergency Rule 1. If it will help and do no harm, call in the cops. These are two men I'd like to see hanged."

"I'm not sure——" she hesitated. "I'm not sure that you're right. If you can hold them yourself, Palfrey might prefer to question them."

Matt's eyes were smiling.

"Yvonne," he said, "you're good, you didn't miss a trick. That's just what I shall do if I can. But rather than let them get away, I'd hand them over to the police. You agree about that?"

"Yes," she said, and caught her breath; but next moment she went on quite normally: "Do you think it was a coincidence that we were here when it happened?"

Matt said: "Meaning, could the fact that we were in the vicinity have leaked out, making the killer act before we could talk to the Carters?"

"Yes."

"Could be," Matt conceded. He glanced along the road again, but nothing was in sight. "I'm going to get an antiseptic dressing for that mosquito bite," he said, and went to the back of the car. Yvonne didn't look round. She was sitting upright in her corner and staring straight ahead when he came back, with a small bottle and some cotton wool in his hand. "I think it's better than it was," he told her. "The swelling's going down."

"Oh, it's nothing, please don't fuss." But she didn't try to stop him from dabbing, and he was very gentle.

"Is there any other road that couple could have taken?" Matt asked.

"No through road, but there are some footpaths."

"That car was a Sunbeam Rapier, or one very like it," Matt asserted and stood back. "It couldn't get along any footpath. Either they've passed here already, or else——"

He broke off, seeing a car turn a corner a long way off. It was coming from the cottages, and the sun glinted on a cream coloured roof and blue sides. He thrust the bottle of antiseptic and the cotton wool into Yvonne's hand, and instead of taking it, she let it fall. It turned on its side in her lap, and a pool of liquid darkened the yellow of her dress and spread swiftly.

"Goddam it, I'm sorry," Matt said, "but they're close by. I'll be back." He rounded the car and took the driving wheel as Yvonne felt for the bottle, and was far too

85

preoccupied with the approaching car to take much notice of her. He swung into the road so that he blocked its whole width, then jumped out. The smaller car was coming fast, but it slowed down and he could hear the faint squeal of brakes.

He saw the two men clearly, one of them bigger and broader than the other, both pale, both obviously scared. They were braced to take the jolt as the car jolted to a standstill, and the smaller of them, at the wheel, was glaring as if at someone he hated.

The other leaned out of his window.

"Get your car off the road, we're in a hurry?"

"Sorry, folk," Matt said. "Maybe you're in too much of a hurry." He didn't smile at them. "Perhaps you could find time to tell me just what happened to the Carters, way back in the valley."

For a split second neither of them moved; before they recovered, Matt showed the small automatic in his right hand. His manner was almost leisurely, but the expression in his eyes told them what would happen if they reached for a weapon or tried to get out. "Just move your car off the road," he ordered, "and stay right there in your seats." He didn't look round, but wished Yvonne would come and join him, a little help would make this much easier. He watched the men as the driver obeyed, and particularly he watched their hands, which were still in sight. Then he glanced swiftly round, but Yvonne hadn't got out.

He felt as if a dagger had stabbed into him.

Stiffness. Fumbling. Slowness of speech. Paralysis. A stroke.

The small car stopped, each man still had his hands in sight, each stared at the small automatic as if they believed that he meant to shoot. He stepped nearer, his own movements stiff and awkward, fear rising in him like lava in a volcano.

"Okay," he said, and squeezed the trigger of the gun.

A soft hissing sound followed, but there was no cloud of vapour, no bullet, no splash of flame; but invisible gas which Palfrey preferred to use. Each of the men seemed to rear up in his seat, and one actually opened his mouth to scream. The scream was cut short as he slumped down.

Both went quite still.

Matt turned round. Dread was in him, driving out everything else.

Yvonne still sat in the car, with the wide gap between her and the spot where he would sit. One leg was stretched out, and the foot showed, as if she had tried to get out. One hand lay on the door, where the window was open. Her head was resting against the glass of the wide window. Her eyes were wide open, she was trying to say something, her lips were moving and so were the muscles of her slender throat; but no sound came.

"All right," Matt said swiftly. "You don't have to worry. Palfrey knows a treatment." Liar. "He'll get you to doctors who know about it, too. Don't worry."

Yvonne still tried to speak, and her eyes swivelled towards the other car, as if she was telling him not to let the men get away.

"It's okay," he said harshly. "They're having a little sleep." He took her foot and lifted it inside the car, and then eased her into a more comfortable position. "Just sit down there and don't worry." He turned and moved swiftly towards the gatehouse. The gatekeeper was standing outside, as if wondering what was going on, but reluctant to leave his post to find out. "Telephone, quickly," Matt urged, "my friend's been taken ill." He went to the doorway of the gatehouse, and the gatekeeper said at once:

"Yes, of course, I'll call a doctor. Dr Hardy——"

"Needs a specialist," Matt said, and lifted the telephone, knowing that the gatekeeper was worried because no stranger should be inside this little cubby

87

hole; but gatekeepers and rules could be forgotten. "Hallo, operator. Get me London E 1212, please . . . Yes, London E 1212, I'll hold on." He saw a van coming from one of the big buildings inside the factory ground, painted green and with the name of the company written in bright yellow on it: Wide World Foods. He called to the gatekeeper: "Is that Larry Hill?"

"No, sir." The gatekeeper approached the van driver, who was getting out of the little cabin. "Okay, Peters, but you can't get out for a minute. This gent's car is in the way."

"I'll take a look," said the man named Peters. He spoke in a nasal, Cockney voice, and offhandedly, as if he wasn't interested in "gents" or in their cars. As he strolled towards the open gates a man spoke into the telephone.

"This is Jim speaking, who's there?"

Matt said with soft urgency: "Matt Stone. I've a couple of men here we ought to talk to, but I don't know that I can handle them."

"Where are you?"

"Outside Wide World Foods——"

"As for the van driver named Peters. He's on the look out for you," Jim said. "What else?"

Matt said: "Yvonne Brown had a mosquito bite. Then she had a stroke."

There was a barely noticeable pause before the man named Jim said: "Wait a minute." He would be talking to Palfrey of course, in that large underground room, and the giant Andromovitch would probably be sitting with him, or else in a room close by.

Suddenly Jim spoke again. "Sap will come down himself. We'll arrange for a ward at the Lauriston Hospital, take Yvonne along. They'll have instructions, and by the time you get there they'll be expecting you. That all?"

"The Carters were burned to death in an attack an hour ago. My prisoners did it. I think Hill might be attacked next."

"Do whatever you think will save him, and get quick results."

"Thanks," Matt said.

"Don't leave the district until Palfrey arrives unless it's essential," Jim added. "Goodbye."

Matt rang off, smoothed down his hair, and felt cold sweat on his forehead, although the afternoon was hot for England: high in the seventies. The gatekeeper was standing in the doorway, completely bewildered. Matt said: "Thanks a lot, I'll see you," and went out, making the gatekeeper stand aside. A short, broad-shouldered man was standing in the gateway, surveying the Chrysler which was blocking his path; his van was level with the gatehouse. As Matt drew level, he said:

"I'm Peters," and spread his hands with the Z5 sign.

"Fine. Can you take care of the couple in the Sunbeam Rapier?"

"Yes. Anything else?"

"Not right now. When you've got them safe, go to Hill's cottage."

Peters had a big, chunky face and a massive chin. He gave a half smile, and said:

"Fine." He didn't ask a question about the girl in the car, but went straight back to his van. By the time he reached it Matt was already in the Chrysler, with Yvonne sitting in it, motionless. She tried to look towards him but could not turn her head.

"The way I told you is right," Matt said. "Palfrey is on his way right now. He's making arrangements at the local hospital for you. Just take it easy."

She stared straight ahead of her.

Matt drove fast, wondering viciously what kind of a fool a man could be. She knew as much as he: that first Jane Hill and afterwards six of the Z5 members had been stricken, as she had been: and that at least three had died.

It took him eight minutes to reach the hospital.

"Yes," said a porter and a youthful-looking doctor,

who were waiting on the steps, "we are all ready for you, we'll take care of Miss Brown now."

Then attendants came hurrying with a stretcher.

Matt said: "There's a lump on her forehead, it was much bigger an hour ago. A mosquito bite swelling. The collapse came soon after that."

"We'll check," the young doctor promised, and watched as the attendants took the girl out of the car with great skill and gentleness. "Where'd she get it?"

"At a place called Oak Hill."

"Bit high for skeeters, I should have thought," the doctor said, then turned his attention to Yvonne. He put a hand on hers as she was carried up the steps and he walked beside her. "You needn't worry at all, Miss Brown, we've caught this very quickly. You simply needn't worry."

He was lying, of course.

That was just soothing syrup.

Was she going to die?

When Matt reached the factory entrance again, the Sunbeam Rapier was still there, but it was empty. Peters and his van were out of sight. Matt got out of the car and went slowly towards the gatehouse; the gatekeeper was on the telephone. Matt lit a cigarette, slowly, steadily; there was a twinge of stiffness at his elbow, and he winced; it went immediately. His mind wasn't working as quickly as he would have liked. He stared at the factory buildings, some big sheds, one of them marked: Canned Goods Warehouse. Larry Hill worked in the main warehouse, loaded his van from there, made his deliveries from there, went back when the day's work was done.

The gatekeeper put down the receiver and leaned forward.

"You all right, sir?"

"Fine, thanks. Larry Hill still here?"

"Yes, sir. He won't be going out again today. He's only an emergency driver. Works mostly in the warehouse."

"Is it right he had a mate?"

"Yes, it—how did *you* know, sir?"

"I get around. Give a message to Larry's mate, will you?"

"Yes, glad to, sir."

"Thanks. Tell him that the sap's rising in the trees near the cottage," Matt said, and his grin drove away the other's look of bewilderment. He passed over a ten shilling note. "Crazy, isn't it?" he said, "but just do that."

"I won't forget, sir."

"Thanks. When would you expect him and Hill to leave?"

"Early today, sir. Five o'clock or so."

"Thanks," said Matt.

A fly buzzed past his face as he spoke, and he didn't take any notice. As he turned, another buzzed very close to him, and he saw a speck pass in front of his eyes but didn't really get a clear view of it. Then he heard a vicious little humming sound: the sound a mosquito would make.

He slapped at one as it passed the end of his nose.

The gatekeeper said: "Are you sure you're all right, sir?"

Matt said gruffly: "Sure, I'm fine. Thanks for your trouble officer." He turned and went swiftly towards his own car, his hands clenched tightly and his teeth set. The road was empty in each direction. He sat at the wheel, but didn't start the engine for a moment; he wiped his forehead. He felt cold sweat at his neck and back and shoulders, too, and he shivered suddenly. A wasp hovered at the window and then flew off. A fly was crawling on the windscreen. If that were a mosquito——

Well, it wasn't.

He started off, driving towards the cottages. He did

not know whether anyone had yet found the burned wreckage of the little Austin, or the bodies; but he knew that few cars ever went that way, and they might stay there for hours, unless someone working at the market garden had seen the smoke. He lit another cigarette, then drove very slowly. Soon he passed the end of the road along which he had driven with Yvonne. The iceberg, the girl with the classic profile.

He pictured her trying desperately to speak to him.

He reached the outskirts of the Forest of Conne, and the gloom beneath the trees. Here and there sunbeams shone through and turned the foliage to a miracle of light and the grass to beauty, but for the most part it was very shadowy. He didn't go fast. He came upon the tunnel, where thick branches, heavy with foliage, intertwined overhead, but he was not thinking so much of that as of the mosquitoes which might breed here. He saw a little patch of soggy, boggy ground, and there was a pool no more than a yard across at one spot quite near the road. The sun was shining nearby, and in the reflection of its light he could see a myriad of tiny insects breaking the surface of the pool; as mosquitoes might. Looking more closely, he saw that they were much tinier than mosquitoes, like tiny moving specks of dust, with a few mosquitoes among them.

He didn't give either of those a second thought, but looked back at the pool.

"I'm crazy," he told himself.

But he wasn't: it was like a dust cloud over the pool. It frightened him.

He felt easier when he was through the tunnel of trees and in that part of the forest where the foliage was thick enough to let the sun give it brightness, but his spirits didn't really rise. He saw a cottage on the outskirts of Conne village, then came upon the thirty miles an hour sign. He slowed down. Outside a row of cottages several children were playing, one of them was waving a hand in front of his face as if to keep mosquitoes or flies away.

And he saw a tiny cloud, rather like a spiral of dark smoke.

Matt's jaw hurt, he was clenching his teeth so hard.

Then he saw a child scratching its cheek, and could see a red blotch like the one which had appeared on Yvonne's forehead.

Should he send the child into Lauriston, with an urgent message for the young doctor?

Was he justified in raising any kind of alarm?

Was there any reason to believe that, even if the mosquitoes and the "dust" were causing this paralysis, there was any known way of minimizing the effect?

He stopped the car at a telephone kiosk, went to it, put in his pennies and then dialled the number of the hospital. When the operator answered, he said very clearly:

"A special patient has just been taken into an isolation ward. I want the doctor in charge informed that a child showing the same early symptoms was seen playing at Merville Cottages, Conne village. Will you make sure that he gets the message quickly?"

"Yes, sir, at once," the operator said promptly. "May I tell him who is calling?"

"That'll be all," Matt said.

He got out of the kiosk. He told himself that it was crazy, that he couldn't be at all sure of the cause of the infection. The shock of what had happened since lunch, from the attack in the car to the seizure which had stricken Yvonne, was preying on his mind. He needed a stiff whisky, would be much more himself then. He went back to the car and started the engine—and a mosquito settled on the inside of the windscreen.

"Brute!" He slapped his hand on the windscreen

93

and killed the thing; this time there was no red smear on glass or window. He looked about the car almost furtively, for fear of seeing more, but saw none: and saw none of that flying dust. That didn't mean a thing.

He drove towards the cottages, for he had studied a map of the neighbourhood and knew exactly which turnings to take. He went slowly, making sure that he missed nothing, and then came in sight of the tiled cottage, with the massed beds of flowers looking much more vivid from here. He could see how well kept it was on the outside, and much labour was put into the garden. He looked beyond it but saw no sign of smoke, no other house, and a clump of trees, oak and beech, where he thought that the little Austin had been burned. He drove past Hill's cottage, glancing at the closed mullioned windows, the closed front door. It was imagination of course, but he had a feeling that it was deserted. He quickened his pace and in five minutes reached the trees.

There was the burned-out wreck of the car.

There were the burned bodies.

And here, beneath the trees, the insects of the countryside darted and hovered and hummed and swooped; and were silent. He saw no spiral of dust nearby.

If it was true that these people had died because the one had seen and the other heard about Jane Hill's symptoms, then it seemed certain that Larry Hill was in equal danger.

It was nearly five o'clock.

He would soon be back to an empty cottage, for his sister had taken his son away.

Matt drove just past the cottage, got out of the car and stood looking at the tiny home, looking soft and beautiful in the late afternoon sunlight. Only the insects and the birds moved, and the air seemed alive with insects and their humming, so that he felt a fear as great as any he had known. Then he saw that one of the windows was open an inch or two. He pushed the small gate back and went along the stone path, where tiny weeds were showing, past the lawns which had looked so trim and neat but which needed mowing; there was a touch of neglect upon this cottage. Matt drew closer to the front door. He heard only those soft, soothing sounds. He neared the window and saw half a dozen little specks on the inside of one of the small panes.

Specks?

They were mosquitoes, *inside* the cottage.

And there were tiny patches of dark dust which looked as if it was smeared on the panes. But one moved suddenly, as if a breath of wind had stirred it, and a "dust" cloud vanished into the room.

10. The Cottage

MATT stood motionless, staring at the specks; and none of these moved. Slowly, he looked at other panes of glass, and saw that there were mosquitoes and the round smears on them, too; the rays of the sun struck the window in such a way that he could see everything clearly.

On that one window alone there must be hundreds of mosquitoes and countless of those flying specks.

Thousands. Millions?

Something buzzed past his eyes. He flinched and struck at the air, and touched something which flew away. He put his hand to his forehead swiftly but felt nothing there; but he shivered. He backed away slowly, as if he dared not turn his back, in case the insects and the specks swarmed after him. He studied the flowers and the bees which hummed about them, and the countless insects there, and he could not make out any mosquitoes or dust, but there were bound to be some. He put his hand on the post of the gate, to open it, and at the side saw a mosquito, as if it were ready to take off. He snatched his hand away, and the wind of the movement sent the insect flying, so that he lost sight of it.

He went round to the back of the car and opened the boot, as he had for the antiseptic. Possibly the application of something very strong might prove an antidote if it were put on quickly enough. He wasn't after that, then. He travelled widely in the car, often staying in small villages overnight, and often finding mosquitoes or flies worrying him; and he kept a small tin of *Quick Kill*, with a spray top. He took this out of a small case. The tin was painted bright red, and the name was in black. He had seen insects drop by the dozen when sprayed with this; would these drop, too? He peered along the road but saw no sign of a van or a car or bicycles. No one had come to see the burned bodies yet—and burned bodies seemed unimportant now. He went back along the path, making himself move more quickly, and trying to ignore the fact that there were so many tiny creatures humming and buzzing and swarming. There were those tiny dust spirals, too. He went close to the window, and did not think that any of the insects had moved. He went close enough to be able to spray through the two-inch gap at the side of the window. The side of the frame hid the menace, but did not stop him from spraying.

He pressed the plastic top of the *Quick Kill* tin, very slowly. The spray hissed gently out. If he was too close, it would set the insects flying, and there would be a hopeless task.

Gently.

The spray was a faint grey colour, rather like smoke. None of the mosquitoes seemed to move, nor did the specks. He kept close to the window for at least three minutes and then backed away and stared at the outside of the window.

Quick Kill should do its job in five minutes; the makers boasted two. It must be five minutes since he had covered that window and yet none had fallen.

A mosquito fell.

A tiny smear of dust disappeared, falling in a tiny shower.

Matt caught his breath and waited tensely; he saw others fall one after the other. He felt a fierce surge of excitement, and hugged the tin as if it were precious beyond words. He waited several more minutes, and by that time all of the insects close to the open section of the window had gone, but several were on panes further away and out of reach of the spray; and little clusters were on sections of the window that were closed. It seemed as if each mosquito had a swarm of tiny satellites, invisible one at a time, but usually in clusters.

"But we can kill them off," he said in a whisper.

He heard the sound of a car engine, not far off. It couldn't be Palfrey yet, of course, but it might be Peters, or it might be Hill and his mate, coming by car. Palfrey had laid a great deal on, but hadn't thought it necessary—or else had not thought it wise—to confide in him, Matthew Stone, about the Z5 men at the food plant.

Remember, Palfrey always knew what he was doing, but——

He set the doubt aside and peered towards the village. On the narrow road through fields of crops he saw a small car. He believed that it was the Sunbeam Rapier he had seen here before: the killer car. It was coming slowly, and he couldn't understand why. Then he saw it swerve towards the right, and a crash seemed inevitable. The Carters' car had gone like this too. This one straightened out, but soon veered towards the other side.

It swung off the road and into a ditch. The front wheels and the radiator disappeared, the back wheels were spinning in the air. There was no sound, and no other sign of movement except these ceaselessly spinning wheels.

The car was at least half a mile away.

He ran to the Chrysler, took the wheel, and swung towards the other car. It took him only a minute or two to reach it. It was an older car than he'd thought. No one had climbed out. The wheels were spinning more slowly now, as if they were tired of the senseless whirl. As he drew up, he jumped out and ran towards the ditch.

A man he had never seen before was trying to crawl out of the car, but could not move. Another, whom he recognized from photographs as Larry Hill, was leaning sideways in his seat, eyes wide open and terror in them.

These two had also been struck down.

It was impossible to straighten the car, a wrecker's van was needed, first to lift and then to drag it out of the ditch. There were the helpless men and the wheels now still, and a faint splashing sound, and earth fell from the side of the ditch into the water at the bottom. Matt was going down. He could stand ankle deep in water, and with luck be able to ease first one man and then the other out of the car, on to the side of the road. They had to be taken to hospital quickly; if they weren't they wouldn't have a chance.

Had they one now?

Matt stepped cautiously because the ditch was steep, and it would not help if he fell in, and he called: "Okay, I'm coming." At least they knew that he was going to try to help. He dislodged a little more earth, and then looked down into the water at the bottom of the ditch, hoping to find a firm spot on which to stand.

He did not.

But he saw several dozen mosquitoes rising off the

surface of the dark, brackish-looking water, some of them skimming the surface itself, some rising a foot or more in the air. And hovering close to them were those little satellites.

If he stepped among them, if he stayed here, he would be bitten; and if he were, he would probably die.

He couldn't hope to cope here with the *Quick Kill*, the mosquitoes and the clouds were in a dozen different places.

He stared, petrified, and tried to make his mind work clearly. He had long been used to the idea of death, and to the idea of dying for Z5 and the half-obscure, half-uttered ideals and hopes which lay in the minds of men whom Palfrey had welded into the world-wide organisation. He had to accept death once it became inevitable; but should he stay here? Should he take the risk of dying, even the risk of losing his power of movement and of speech?

He was first and last a member of Z5, and working for it. It was essential to report everything he had found out to Palfrey, who might find in it all that was needed to kill the horror. He had to keep himself alive at least until he was able to warn the villagers at Conne not to come here. The whole village, the whole area, had to be isolated.

All these things went through his mind in a fragment of time, and while he saw the hovering insects and the foot of Larry Hill's companion. The man was staring at him, pleading.

Matt said in a strangled voice:

"I'll get help."

He saw two mosquitoes settle on the man's forehead, then dust, in tiny dark circles. There was nothing the other man could do about it, not even brush them off. Then a mosquito settled on Matt's own right hand. He slapped and squashed it, blew at it desperately, then turned and leapt up the bank.

The awful reproach in the other's eyes was there to haunt him.

He reached the wheel of his own car. There was room to pass. He got in and took the wheel; and there was a mosquito on the inside of the windscreen; he should have kept the windows closed. Where there was one there might be dozens. He squashed the one and no blood showed, and no dust either. He looked round at the cream-coloured upholstery and the windows, the uprights, everywhere, and saw nothing to fear and heard no buzzing. As he started off he could not stop himself from glancing towards the wrecked car. The men were nearly hidden from him, but he saw that Larry Hill had slumped further away.

He began to put on speed. A wasp bumped against one of the ventilation windows and fell inside the car close to his foot. He snatched his foot off the accelerator. Tight-lipped, he closed the ventilation windows. The sun shone hot upon the glass and he began to sweat, but he kept the windows closed.

Then, suddenly, tiny black specks dotted the windscreen; then came dark dust, covering it as if he'd driven over a dirt road.

Understanding came swiftly.

He had flown through a cloud of the mosquitoes and their satellites.

He could just make out spirals of them, clear against the sky. Dozens more mosquitoes appeared on the glass, tiny, dead insects, which might carry death and coma with them. He gritted his teeth so hard that his jaws hurt, but soon he had passed through this cloud, and no additional specks came onto the glass. But the dust remained. At any other time he would have stopped, got out and cleaned the windscreen, but he could not bring himself to do that now.

He approached the village.

He was aware of a stillness which had not been

100

there when he had come through; an absolute lack of movement. He had seen two people working in their gardens here; seen others in the street, inside the village shops, but no one was about, it was like a village which had gone to sleep. He slowed down. A cycle lay on its side, on the pavement, and he saw that the front wheel was buckled where it had crashed against the wall of a cottage. The door of the cottage was wide open and he could see the furniture inside, the polished linoleum, some china hanging on the wall. He passed another shop and saw a man sitting back against the shelves filled with cans of food; a man whose eyes were open but who seemed to be sitting motionless.

Matt passed the post office.

One of the small red vans of the postal service had crashed into a scarlet pillar box outside the little sub-office. Inside, the driver was leaning aginst the counter, with his right hand stretched out, as if he was trying to get something; and his lips were working but no sound came from them.

Matt saw the row of cottages and the playing children, but they were no longer playing. The most awful thing was of the child who sat against the closed doorway of a cottage, eyes wide open in mute appeal, body limp and helpless.

"Oh, God," Matt said in a fierce voice. "Oh, God, how can I stop it, how can I stop it?"

He must go on.

He must make sure that no one came to the village unprepared, but now there was an awful fear in his mind; a fear that this plague had spread already, that it had reached Lauriston. Why not? Which way was the wind? He stared at the trees and the hedges on the far side of the village, and he shouted aloud:

"Which way is the wind?"

He couldn't tell from the moving car; one never could. Did it matter whether he knew or not? He had to get a warning through. He was twelve miles or more from Lauriston, he had to drive through the forest, and the forest might be alive with these plague carriers. Remember, he had to see Palfrey and had to get a warning through, for other people would be driving along this road, as the post office driver had.

He turned a corner.

A motor-cyclist was lying on the road close to the hedge, and his machine was propped up against the hedge; he had had time to do that. There was a red smear on his forehead, no doubt he had squashed a mosquito. He still had the strength to wave an appeal for help. Ignoring it was like ignoring the cry of a child in pain.

Matt turned another corner, and the road stretched straight for half a mile. He made himself slow down and tried to think dispassionately. He would have to telephone the warning, could not allow more people to come to the village and be struck down. He must contact the police, Palfrey and Z5. He must turn back to the village and telephone, there was not likely to be a phone between here and the forest.

Turn *back*.

He saw a gateway, stopped, reversed into it, and started back. Then he said: "You lunatic," and drove more swiftly, past the motor-cyclist again; the man was no longer able to wave. He pulled up outside the post office in this village of silence, and then turned round and stretched out for the tin of *Quick Kill*, which was in the pocket of one of the rear doors. Next he opened his door swiftly and stepped out, then slammed the door to make sure that nothing could get in. He was only a step from the kiosk. He saw the mosquitoes, with their terrifying attendants, at the window. They were both inside and out; and at the window of the shop also. None seemed to be flying near him. He pulled open the heavy door of the kiosk, kept it open with his foot and sprayed the *Quick Kill* in. Two or three mosquitoes flew about in front of him, disturbed by his movements, and he kept waving his arms about to try to make sure that they didn't settle. He couldn't see anything else, but the flying dust wouldn't always show up.

He saw the mosquitoes beginning to fall inside the kiosk, waited for another minute, and then stepped in himself. There were a dozen or more insects on the black prepayment box, apparently dead; and dozens on the floor and on the frames of the little windows. He dialled 999 for the emergency, and wondered whether there was a village exchange and whether the operator would be at her switchboard.

No one answered.

Why don't they answer?

A girl asked for his number in a detached voice: he gave 999. Then she asked: "Do you want Police, Fire or Ambulance."

"Police, in a hurry," Matt stared at the inside of the post office. Two women were in there, eyes open, bodies helpless, one on the floor, one on a chair. Their faces seemed dirty: smeared as with dust.

"This is Lauriston Police Station, can I help you?" Matt said. "Superintendent on duty, please. Reference Z5."

"Who wants——" there was a pause, then an almost startled: "Did you say Z5?"

"Yes. Hurry."

"One moment please, sir."

It was a long moment, even though the code had worked; the code to use only in desperate emergency. No one would ever question the wisdom of this.

A man spoke.

"Superintendent Collis speaking. Who is that, please?"

"Superintendent," Matt said, very slowly and deliberately, "I am speaking from Conne village. There is a plague of mosquitoes here, and their bite seems to be

103

fatal. They are accompanied by a kind of dust. That's the only way I can describe it, but it's deadly. It is absolutely essential to isolate the village, making sure no one comes in unless they are fully protected."

"One moment sir," the superintendent said, and Matt could have cursed him. But probably he thought he was talking to a madman; anyhow, the next thing would be a polite "I'll see to it, sir," and then silence.

Another man said: "Is that you, Matt?"

It was Palfrey.

"All right, take it easy," Palfrey said two minutes afterwards, and the calmness of his manner was like a benediction. "The police will take emergency action and cordon the area off. Civil Defence units will come into it, wearing protective clothing, and we'll assume it's a form of gas or bacteriological assault. We can cope, anyhow. Do you know how far beyond Conne they've spread?"

"No. I came about a mile and a half out of the village on the Lauriston side, and they were at least two miles on the Hills' cottage side. Hill and a man with him were ditched, and badly bitten."

"All right, Matt," Palfrey said. "I'll fix it. The police are already putting up road blocks on the outskirts of Lauriston, just beyond the factory, to keep traffic out of the area. It's a fairly easy place to isolate, with the hills all round it. Where are you speaking from?"

"The telephone booth outside the post office."

"Free of the things?"

"I had some *Quick Kill* handy. It seems to work, but when the dust really swarms——" Matt broke off.

"Can you get to your car safely?"

"I think so."

"Drive to the Forest Hotel and stop about half a mile away," Palfrey said. "I'll have someone there to decon-

104

taminate your car. Then go on to the hotel. If it's free from the swarms we'll be able to meet there. If it's not, stay with a decontamination squad until you get further orders. There's one positioned near the hotel."

"Listen, Sap, the people here need help."

"You can't help them any more, but we might be able to. Don't try being a hero."

"All right," Matt muttered.

"And, Matt," said Palfrey quickly, "you've done quite a job."

He rang off.

Matt stood inside the tiny kiosk. He was sticky and hot, and those last words of Palfrey's hadn't really made much difference. He could see the mosquitoes and the dust on the outside of the window, and his car seemed to be yards away, not just a foot or two. He made to make a dash for it. He took the handle and got ready to push; pushed the door back and streaked across the pavement to his car, jerked that door open, and slid inside his seat. The door slammed. He looked round, almost desperately, fearfully; had any got in? He took the *Quick Kill* from his pocket and sprayed the car. The smell was unpleasant, but at least it gave him a feeling of security.

He drove on steadily.

Security?

If it was gas or bacteria, what good would *Quick Kill* do? He'd seen it work, but the effect might only be temporary.

Two miles out on the Lauriston Road he saw a signpost reading: *To Forest Hotel.* That way, he could reach it more quickly. A narrow paved road ran through open country at first, but soon he was on the edge of the forest, and could see the massed trees a mile or two ahead. The sun shining on them, from this position, made them seem more golden than green, and he had seldom seen greater beauty. There was peacefulness too; the green of the trees and grass, the soft blue of the sky, here and there a fleck of white clouds, everything that went to make England's pleasance, which he had heard so much about and had only now learned to love. This was so different from the Arizona desert that it was hard to believe that such a place as Phoenix existed in the same world as this.

Soon he was among the trees.

He had not yet seen any dark spirals of dust or the mosquitoes, and no more had come on to his windscreen. He felt more relaxed, and knew that it was partly due to the fact that Palfrey had reassured him; at least the authorities were trying to cope. He tried to strengthen his reassurance. This part of England could easily be isolated, as Palfrey had said, and once the authorities were warned of the danger, surely they could cope. If there was an outbreak of this horror in one of the Arab States, say, or South America, or even parts of North America, it would be hell. He remembered a plague of mosquitoes in New Orleans, driven by an unusual wind off the Mississippi swamps. That plague had lasted for nearly a month.

But the satellite dust was something new.

Bacteriological warfare? Was this how it would start? This wasn't New Orleans, there were no swamps nearby.

Dust began to leap on to his windscreen.

His nerves grew taut in a moment. His teeth clenched again. He was close to the edge of the forest and it was darker beyond, but he could see the little black marks of mosquitoes, not so many as before, but more than enough; and he saw a big spiral of dust, like a small desert whirlwind of black sand. The sun glinted on water. He knew that he had made at least one mistake. It was swampy land.

A hundred yards further on there was a clearing, and drawn off the road, a small car. On the grass, one in a chair, the others lying in a heap, was a man and two women. He felt quite sure that they had been bitten and struck down.

He drove on.

He would forever hate himself, after this day.

Then, perhaps a mile away at the end of a long, straight road through the forest, he saw a cyclist; and as he drew nearer he saw that it was a girl.

11.   Defiance

SHE came cyling along briskly, and seemed to be completely oblivious of dust, of mosquitoes and of danger. Matt could have shrieked at her. She crossed the path of a beam of sunlight coming through a gap in the branches, and her hair seemed to catch alight; a light auburn, like the girl at the hotel who had served them at luncheon—and like Rondivallo's Maureen O'Shea. Then she came into the shadow again, and all he could see was a young girl wearing a pale green dress, sandals, with nice legs, nice, sunbrowned arms. The waitress. She was pretty, as Matt already knew. He had slowed down, and there was near terror in him, for he saw mosquitoes flying close to the car, and if they were there, then they must be close to the girl who was now no more than fifty yards away from him. She was looking at him, and went towards one side of the road, and Matt realized that he was heading towards her, enough to cause alarm.

He stopped.

He had to open the window.

He opened the ventilation window, leaving little room for any insect to come through, and shouted at the girl:

"Stop, there. Stop!"

107

She heard and obeyed, but looked puzzled. He sat at the wheel, conscious of the death which lurked in the very air, of the fact that he was due to stay in his car until reaching Palfrey's decontamination squad. The girl was now a little wary, and he could see that she was looking at the closed windows, as if realizing how absurd it was to keep them closed on a day as hot as this. She looked quite lovely, with the softness which the sheen of her hair gave her.

Matt opened the door; he could not let her stay out here, could not let another human being be attacked. He got out swiftly, and saw the way her hands tightened on the handlebars; as if she wanted to move off. But he was in the way and she couldn't. Just here, there were mosquitoes, but he saw none of the tiny satellite clouds.

"Get off your bicycle and get in the car," he ordered roughly. "Hurry!"

Her eyes were honey-coloured.

"I'll do no such thing," she said, half angry and half scared. "Move aside now, and let me pass."

The Irish brogue which had been noticeable at luncheon was much more pronounced, and her face was flushed. He didn't need telling why. Here was a lonely forest road, and a man in a powerful car stopping a girl on her own—oh, God, why did it have to be so difficult?

"Listen to me," he said, forcing himself to speak calmly. "There has been an escape of poison gas in the district, and everyone must get under cover. I'm going to a decontamination point now. Get off your bicycle and get into the car."

"It's a fine story you're telling me," she said, and there was a hint of laughter in her voice, although obviously she was a little scared. "It's a new one, I have to say that for you. Now get out of my way, please, I want to get on."

He didn't move.

"I'm quite serious," he said. "There's death in the forest."

Out of the corner of his eyes he caught sight of a few dozen mosquitoes; they flew into a tiny sunbeam, which turned their wings to gold and their bodies to beauty; and they were only two yards away. He could not see any dust. He waved at them.

"It's a madman you are," the girl said, and her laugh took on a note of real nervousness. "Please let me pass."

Instead, he stepped towards her, hands stretched out to hold the bicycle. She slapped at his right hand, then trod heavily on the pedal and shot forward. He was taken so much by surprise that he moved. She thrust her hand out to push him further away. He lost his balance and staggered; and she was past him, cycling furiously towards the village of silence, and to all the horrors there.

"Come back!" he shouted. "Come back!"

She glanced over her shoulder, cycling furiously. The only way to catch up with her was to turn the car. The little fool deserved anything she got, he couldn't have warned her more clearly.

She didn't look where she was going and the front wheel touched the side of the road, where there was a slight dip; and she pitched forward. As she tried desperately to save herself, Matt went after her; at least she couldn't get away again. She managed to leap from the machine without falling, pushed it away and turned to face him; the expression on his face would have been enough to frighten anyone.

"Don't come near me!" she cried. "Don't come near me!" Her hands were raised to fend Matt off, and he saw her look round desperately, as if for a weapon, or else in hope of seeing someone come to her rescue.

Then a mosquito settled lightly on the side of her arm.

Matt jumped forward, and struck at it. He did not touch it, but the wind of the movement dislodged the insect, which flew off and was lost to sight.

There was no visible dust.

The girl hadn't a chance.

She was terrified now, backing away and stumbling. Matt closed with her, put his arms round her and held her tightly, so that she couldn't struggle or kick. He lifted her clear of the ground, finding that she was rigid with terror. He ran to the car, bundled her in, and slammed the door. She had it open again by the time he was at the wheel, but he dragged her back, leaned across her, and slammed the door. He was gasping for breath, and the girl was pressing against the door so as to keep her distance.

"Relax," he made himself say. "I'm not going to hurt you. You may not believe it, but I'm trying to save your life." He took the *Quick Kill* and sprayed it about the car again, while the girl stared as if he had taken leave of his senses. He put the tin back, and went on: "No, I'm not mad, either. Did that bite you?"

"Did *what* bite me?" She had the slight emphasis on the "h" in what, to make it sound so Irish, and watched him with enormous rounded eyes.

"There was a mosquito on your arm," he said. "Did it bite you?"

"A mosquito, was it? No, I don't think it bit me." She rubbed her arm with her forefinger. "But perhaps it did, there's a little irritation, but it'll do me no harm."

She stopped, and held her breath.

He stared at her, as if in horror; and he felt real horror. For he could see the tiny bump, not yet even red, which was rising just below her right elbow, exactly where the mosquito had been.

"You can think I'm crazy, you can think what you like, but I've got to squeeze the poison out of the bite," Matt said. "Don't make any more fuss. Stretch out your arm."

She didn't move.

110

"Stretch your arm out!" he shouted at her. "Do I have to knock sense into you?"

Terror showed in her eyes, and he could understand that and yet could not control himself because he could not make her believe her danger. Slowly, she held her arm towards him, staring all the time, and he took her wrist with his left hand and was about to squeeze the little bump with his right.

Then, his door opened.

He heard the movement, dropped the girl's arm, and turned his head. A man was at the open door. All Matt really saw was his waist, and a clenched fist moving at great speed. He could not dodge. The blow caught him on the side of the jaw, jolting him sideways. He banged against the windscreen, and for a few moments was so dazed that he could not think about his own or the girl's danger. Then he felt himself being dragged out of the car; he hadn't the strength to resist.

His head began to clear.

He saw the man standing on the grass of the forest, with the massed trees and the little shafts of sunlight showing behind him; a big, handsome fellow wearing a tweed jacket, riding breeches and leather leggings. In his right hand was a sturdy stick, with a sharp ferrule at the end. He was staring across the roof of the car, where the girl was already scrambling out, and there was a faint smile at his lips as he turned back to Matt.

The smile faded; bleakness replaced it.

"Try to give me one reason why I shouldn't thrash the wits out of you," he said.

He looked quite capable of doing that.

The girl appeared from one side, and about them all as they stood by the side of the big car, the insects of the forest hovered and hummed, and not far off a little cloud of mosquitoes was bright in the sun; only a gentle wind was needed to blow them right into their faces.

Matt said: "I'll warn you as I've warned the girl. There

111

is a kind of poison gas loose in the forest, and it's being carried by mosquitoes. I've seen a dozen people paralysed already, and know of some who died. This girl's been bitten by a mosquito."

He turned towards her.

She had lost some colour, and looked distressed. Now she glanced down at her arm; there was just a little whitish bump, not much larger than it had been when she had last seen it. But he had scared her, and she put a hand towards it.

The big man said: "That's the best tale I've heard for a long time. Did he tell you the same story, Kathleen?"

"Yes, sir, he did indeed," Kathleen said.

"Sir." Master and servant?

"I told her the same story and it's as true as I'm standing here."

"You almost make me believe it," the big man said, but he didn't act as if he was even slightly nervous, just smiled broadly at the girl. "Let me see this dangerous bite."

She went forward, with her arm outstretched.

At luncheon, her uniform had hidden her figure, and Matt hadn't been thinking about figures when he had seen her coming towards him on the bicycle; but he couldn't fail to see her more clearly now. The thrust of her high young breasts against the flowered green dress, the way she moved, the rounded beauty of her arm, the pallor of her face and the sunlit auburn of her hair, made her a picture to dream about.

She should soon begin to feel the effect of the poison.

There was one odd thing: she hadn't started to scratch it yet.

And there was no "dust," remember.

The tall man held the girl's hand for a moment, quite

112

impersonally, then let her arm fall. There was a dry twist at his lips as he turned to Matt, and said very slowly and deliberately:

"It looks an ordinary gnat bite to me. You'd better drive on, before I change my mind and knock the nonsense out of you. In this country it's quite safe for a girl to travel alone."

"It won't be safe for her or for you," Matt said. "But when you begin to feel the pain, don't blame me."

"Don't talk like a lunatic." The other's eyes hardened. "Drive on."

"Listen to me," Matt said desperately. "I've arranged for the whole area to be cordoned off. Everyone in Conne village is in a state of collapse, and soon——"

A mosquito hummed close, and he struck at it.

"Oh, get into your car and take your lunatic ideas back home with you," the big man said roughly. He gripped Matt's elbow and pushed him towards the car. "If I have any more of this, I'll lose my patience."

Matt said: "I've never known anyone ask for it more." He stiffened his arm, and the big man seemed to lose his temper, clenching his fist to strike. The girl cried out a name: it sounded like "Mr Lawson!"

The man said: "Get in and drive off."

Matt twisted his arm round and gripped his wrist, then leaned his weight against him. He felt him give way, and twisted. The big man staggered backwards, and the girl cried out again. The man came up against a sapling, and would have fallen but for its support; he looked flabbergasted.

Matt didn't speak as he got into the car and closed the door; but he wound down the window, and called out as he started the engine:

"I hope you get another chance. Get under cover, and make it fast. I'm still prepared to drive you."

The man was glaring at him angrily, and the girl looked as if she didn't know what to do.

Matt drove off.

113

How long would it be before the poison took effect?

He tried to remember how long it had been with Yvonne. It was hard to believe that it had happened on this very day. That they had lunched together and the Irish girl had served them, and then they had driven off, knowing nothing of the horror that lurked in the air.

How long would it be before the girl Kathleen began to feel the paralysis?

And would the man be affected too?

How could he prevent it?

12. The Squad

THE narrow road seemed to go on unendingly, and the forest did not change on either side; for mile after mile it looked the same, here dark and shadowy, there bright as the sun forced its way through the small clearings, here thick with undergrowth, there quite clear, with beech and birch, slender and spreading on either side. Matt felt the wind cold on his forehead for a few minutes, but didn't close the window. He had given way completely to his fears, and one couldn't live on fear.

That crazy fool of a man.

Well, who could blame him, and who could blame anyone? Only when you had seen victims of the bites could you know the real depths of the horror.

When was he going to reach the decontamination squad? Had Palfrey really been able to arrange one? Was Palfrey as good as his reputation, or was he a lot of hot air? He had reached Lauriston swiftly enough, and must have flown from London.

Matt saw a little sign on the side of the road, and as he drew nearer, read: *Danger: Road Up.* He relaxed and almost burst out laughing, it seemed so silly; the ordinary everyday things. *Danger: Road Up. Danger—*

114

Mosquito Bites. Danger—Mad American in Chrysler. Danger—Dust.

He turned the corner and jammed on his brakes, although there was nothing very near. Some fifty yards away a car was drawn up across the road. Near this were several policemen in uniform, all looking a little peculiar. There were two men in plain clothes too, and a motor-cyclist. Other men were taking something off an open truck which was pulled off the road. Matt saw that these were trestles, and realized that they were making a road block. As he drew nearer, at a crawling pace, he saw a large picnic area with *No Litter* signs. Then he saw why the policemen looked odd: muslin hung round their helmets and over their faces. They wore gloves too.

Everyone in sight had the same kind of protection. Matt thought: "Well, Palfrey can work miracles."

He followed a policeman's directions, turned on to the parking field, and stopped. A small green van stood with its rear doors open, and some cylinders, brushes and sprays were inside. A man was taking out a spray which was connected to a long, snaky, plastic pipe about the size of a hosepipe.

Matt opened the door.

"Stay in your car for a moment, please," said the man with the spray. "Close the windows, please."

Matt obeyed.

The man wore rubber gloves, and the muslin, hanging from a steel helmet, protected his face. He pressed a button on the spray and a pale grey vapour spread out, covering the windows and the windscreen, for a minute or more Matt could not see out. Then the other began to rub down the windows and the cellulose with a large sponge; and he squeezed the sponge off into a pail, as if to make sure that dirty moisture was gone. Then he stood back, pointing to the door. Matt opened it and stepped out. In spite of the brightness of the sun it seemed much cooler outside than it had in; he had not

115

realized how hot he was. He stood quite still, looking about; and although he did not fully realize it, he was watching for mosquitoes and their satellite clouds.

"Can't be absolutely sure, sir, but we think it's quite clear round here," the man said. He looked pale and tired behind the muslin. "We've arranged for aircraft to spray the area for a two-mile radius of Forest Hotel, so it should be all right for a while." He turned to his van and picked up a steel helmet with a muslin drape, and a pair of loose-fitting rubber gloves. "Better be safe than sorry, though. Will you put these on?"

Matt said: "Thanks." He had driven at least eight miles since leaving the girl and the man in the forest—six or more beyond the sprayed area. He did not know this man, but his own identity seemed to be taken for granted. "Is there any news from Conne village?"

"Nothing fresh, sir."

"Anything being done about people inside the infected area?"

"Oh yes sir. Special patrols are out, everyone on the telephone is being contacted and told to close all windows and keep indoors. Everything possible's being done, you needn't worry about that."

"Thanks." That was something; but there was the girl Kathleen, with the bite on her arm and the fear and anger in her eyes, her fair auburn hair and her beauty. "Any instructions for me? My name is——"

"Mr Stone, sir, I know. We've been on the look-out for you. You're asked to report to Forest Hotel at once. The doctor will be there."

The doctor?

Palfrey.

Matt felt an easing of depression as he hurried eagerly back to his car. It was as if seeing and talking to Palfrey would ease the almost intolerable burden.

He heard aircraft, and saw one old biplane and a helicopter; spraying. *Was* this a miracle?

Was there any special reason why Palfrey should have taken him so seriously?

The hotel looked almost medieval, approached from this road, with two turrets and part of a castellated wall with arrow slits for windows. A sunken garden showed that there had once been a moat here. Yvonne had told him that the hotel had been built on the site of an old ruin, but he had not realized that the ruin had been reconstructed. The sun was shining on the building, the lawns surrounding it looked fresh and newly-watered, the flower beds reminded him of those at the little cottage not far away; and also reminded him of Larry Hill and the other man in that small car. He drove on a circular drive to the front of the hotel. Somehow it seemed wrong when he saw three gardeners working, including a youth who couldn't be long past school age.

Nothing here suggested crisis.

On one side of the hotel at the front was a verandah with gay umbrellas and awnings, and beneath these sat half a dozen hotel guests, with a young maid bustling about among them. It was farcical. A mile or two away people were dying, some might already be dead, a whole village had been smitten, yet here it could be so placid.

He parked the car next to a silver grey Rolls-Bentley and hurried up the steps leading to the verandah and the main hall. The sun was hot on the back of his head, he was sticky with sweat, he wanted a shower, above all he needed someone to talk to. Closer to the guests, he saw their look of tension: it was evident in the maid's manner too. Matt strode into the hall, which was cool and shadowy, and a youthful-looking man was standing at the foot of the big, dark oak staircase; one whom he hadn't seen before.

"You're Matt Stone," this man said.

117

"That's right."

"I'm a Sapper! The great man's in a main front bedroom on the first floor. Room 7. Turn right at the head of the stairs and then turn left."

"Thanks," Matt said.

He hurried up; he couldn't get to Palfrey too soon. No one else was about when he reached the door of Room 7, tapped sharply, then tried the handle. The door was locked, and that shouldn't have surprised him. He heard a movement inside the room, and the door was opened by a small, knuckly-looking man with a close-cropped head. This man stood aside.

"Come in."

"Thanks." Matt squeezed through the doorway opening and noticed that the door was closed very quickly behind him; almost as if there was fear, after all, that the mosquitoes would get in here. Then he saw Palfrey sitting at a table in a bay window which overlooked the front steps, the main drive and the forest; the lovely view that he had seen with Yvonne. She had been so cold and distant at the time that he had disliked her acutely, but now he felt choky whenever he thought of her.

Palfrey had masses of papers in front of him and two telephones by his side, but as Matt drew up he glanced round, said: "Half a tick," and scribbled on a slip of paper, then called: "Sarak, take this down, will you?" and handed the slip of paper to the knuckly man. Then he pushed his chair back and turned to Matt.

"Been hell, hasn't it?" he said, in his quiet voice. "I want to hear all about it, in detail, but if there's anything specially on your mind, let me know now." He bent down and took a whisky bottle from a cabinet at his side, and a glass; and a small bowl of ice. "On the rocks?"

Matt said heavily: "Sure, on the rocks." He watched the lumps of ice go in, heard them clink against the

118

glass, saw the straw-coloured Scotch whisky fall over them in a miniature cascade. "Thanks," he said. "I'm beginning to understand why they made you the boss." He had never wanted a drink so much. "Ah! Any news of Yvonne Brown?"

"Only that she's in good hands."

"Larry Hill?"

"I've just heard that he's been picked up, and that he and the man with him are on their way to Lauriston Hospital, where a special wing has been set aside for these cases. Specialists are coming down from London."

"Have the Carters been identified for certain?"

"Not yet, but I think they will be."

"I saw that happen." Matt said slowly, and sipped his drink. "I saw two men fling fire bombs at them, and the car burst into smoke and flames. Did you know that Peters had caught——"

"Oh yes," said Palfrey, and he offered cigarettes and then a lighter. "The two men have talked—I saw them as soon as I reached Lauriston. They are both known criminals with a record of violence. They say that they were paid five hundred pounds to attack the Carters and set the car on fire, and were paid in advance. They had the money with them. How much is anyone's guess, but they won't say more.

"Do they——"

"Know anything about the mosquitoes? They say they don't," said Palfrey. "They're among the very few people to get out of the infected region without being affected." His gaze was very direct as he said that, and he put a hand to a few strands of hair at his forehead.

Matt said thickly: "Know how many casualties?"

"No, but certainly hundreds," Palfrey was almost pedantic. "Most are probably from Conne itself. We haven't had reports from all the outlying hamlets, the woodmen's cottages and the isolated houses, but they keep coming in. The total number of estimated casualties is over five hundred. None of the people who've been telephoned within the area has replied, and the assumption is that they can't."

Matt said: "Give me another drink."

"Of course," said Palfrey. "And if I were you I'd take a shower after that. Your luggage has gone up, and you can take time off." He was calm and detached; too calm. He poured out. "Just to keep you right in the picture, once we suspected gas or bacteria, we called on the county and military air civil defence forces. As soon as we knew that mosquitoes appeared to be carrying the plague, with these satellite insects, we arranged for the whole area to be sprayed from the air, decontamination posts set everywhere, and everything possible was done. With luck, the outbreak's been confined."

Matt pushed his glass away.

"I could do with that shower right now. Will it be all right if I tell you my story afterward?"

"During the shower," Palfrey said. "Sarak can take over here." He broke off when a telephone bell rang, and lifted the receiver very quickly: as if afraid that it would bring bad news. "Palfrey," he said, and added abruptly: "Yes, Stefan?"

Stefan Andromovitch, from London.

"Yes," Palfrey said again.

He did not make a note and did not look away from the far wall; all he did was to set his lips as he listened; and that brought Matt almost to screaming point, because it was so obvious that this was news of grave importance. Bad news?

Palfrey didn't speak for at least half a minute; then he said:

"So the time between the first symptoms and death is down to two hours in some cases . . . Yes . . . Yes, I'd heard that our man in Buenos Aires was dead, that's a clean sweep of them all," He glanced swiftly at Matt, as if to make sure that he understood the significance of that. "I think we'd better advise the strongest civil defence precautions in each area, treating the mosquito satellite cloud as bacteriological in nature . . . What?"

He seemed to go very tense. Then he relaxed. "Hm," he said, as if disappointed. "Well, we must have Mitchison ready to pounce. Right, Stefan . . . Yes, he's here and seems all right . . . Yes."

He rang off.

Matt was standing and staring tensely, and Palfrey was looking up, a few strands of hair making an absurd little curl at his forehead, his shoulders rounded, the look of weakness upon him.

"You heard most of that, I fancy," he said, "It was a week or more before Jane Hill died. Now death has followed within two hours of the symptoms." He paused. "Not in every case so far, thank God. It's possible that there will be an outbreak of the plague wherever Rondivallo has been. What I want to know above everything else is why our chaps were killed. I thought Korven was on the point of a discovery, but there was no indication that the others were. There's a report from Budapest that our man there had a unfamiliar growth, fungoid in nature, on his larynx before he died, but there's not been time for an autopsy. The report is being checked in other victims as far as it can be," Palfrey paused, and then added abruptly: "There isn't any clue about Rondivallo's present hiding-place. No use asking you if you found any."

"I didn't," Matt said abruptly. "I haven't even proved that he was in the district."

"He was here, at this hotel, until three months ago." Palfrey stood up, almost an uncoiling process. "Come and have that shower, and let me hear exactly what happened from the time you first arrived." He glanced at the knuckly man, who had been back for several minutes. "Take over, Sarak, will you?"

"At once, yes," the man said. He nearly made it "vonce" and "ess," and obviously English wasn't his native language; middle European, Matt thought. He went

121

across to the bathroom, which was large, luxurious, and tiled green. Two bathrobes hung behind the door, with several thick towels. Matt stripped, stepped into the bath and switched on the shower cautiously; every little everyday action was a help. The water hissed. He began to talk, and Palfrey sat on a stool in the doorway, asking a question now and then.

Matt switched off the water.

"Want a towel?" Palfrey tossed one. "This waitress you saw later in the Forest. You say she looked very like Maureen O'Shea, Rondivallo's girl friend."

"By description, she might have been the same girl," said Matt. "When I compared her with the photograph of Maureen O'Shea, I could see that she wasn't. I'd say she was a sister."

"Named Kathleen. Hmm."

"Sap," Matt said quietly, "what difference does it make? She was bitten. I saw the damned brute on her arm. If the man hadn't interrupted I might have been able to get the poison out."

"Could be," Palfrey said, as Matt finished drying himself, and stretched out for one of the bathrobes. "She is a sister of Maureen O'Shea, and came here to work a month or so after Maureen disappeared—about the same time as Rondivallo disappeared. That much we know. By your description the man in the forest was Kurt Larsen, who owns the hotel. He's an Anglo-Swede who's been here for several years." Palfrey stood up abruptly. "We can't try to keep anything under cover now, we've got to come right out into the open in the search for Rondivallo." He went on with quiet, telling vehemence. "We have to find him, because he's our only real line of inquiry on this plague of silence. If this thing could happen here as quickly and suddenly as it did, what would happen if a larger town was invaded? What would happen if London was?" He led the way into the big room, still talking in a low-pitched voice, and approached the big bay window, with the beautiful, panoramic view beyond. "We've got to find Rondivallo. We've got to find how the mosquitoes and the satellites become infected. We can kill the mosquitoes once we know where they are, but we don't know where the larvas are. We don't know where they might be breeding at this very minute, and we don't yet know what this 'dust' is. We can guess that Mrs Hill was bitten, and that the two doctors were killed because they examined her soon after the seizure. The fact that trouble always starts in the throat and this new fungoid growth found on a infected larynx, might be related. But that's as far as we can go. We may only have a little while to work in Matt. This could soon get absolutely out of control."

Matt said huskily: "I didn't know I could be so scared."

"We can be scared," Palfrey said, and smiled faintly. "Now we've got to start questioning every one who knew Maureen O'Shea, everyone on the staff and the managements, everyone who was here when Rondivallo stayed here."

He glanced away from Matt towards the window, and instead of turning back, stopped speaking and stared.

Matt darted forward.

He saw the waitress, Kathleen O'Shea, cycling along the outer circular drive, obviously going towards the back of the hotel and the servants' quarters. The sun was shining on her lovely hair, on the green dress, on her slim arms and legs.

Palfrey said softly: "Are you sure that she was bitten?"

"Quite sure," Matt said, and his voice was hoarse with unbelief.

13. Kathleen O'Shea

PALFREY studied Matthew Stone's face.

He had known Stone for a long time, and the reports which had come after the screening to which he'd been subjected before entering the service of Z5 had been remarkable. There was no member with better qualifications or a finer record. He was the son of a wealthy newspaperman in the Middle West of the United States, and his interest in journalism had first started his travels and now gave a sound excuse for them. He could go anywhere as a newspaperman and be accepted. He had been in the heart of a dozen trouble centres, including the Middle East and Eastern Europe, during fierce troubles there, and had shown an absolute courage allied to a quick understanding of the factor involved. He had a remarkable memory for events of all kinds and an insatiable thirst for information, as well as the courage and determination to keep trying to get what he wanted.

Few of his qualities ever showed on his face; he was a pleasant-looking young American with a crewcut, a clear complexion, keen eyes, an easy laugh, a pleasant, drawling voice which attracted many people.

Above all his other qualifications was the fact that he could stand up to unexpected pressures well: he had once been interrogated by Security Police for eight days without yielding an item of information.

No agent had ever been subjected to greater shocks and pressures than he had during the past few hours. When he had come in here, the effect of the pressures had shown clearly in his eyes, but Palfrey had seen the way he had driven up to the hotel, seen the way he had hurried up the steps, and knew whatever had happened he hadn't been subdued. During their talk he had shown that his nerves had been torn. He had been jerkier in speech than usual, hardly knowing what to do with his hands, but his mind had been clear and the details of his story convincing.

Now, as Palfrey studied him, a new expression chased the unbelief away. He watched the girl cycling until she was out of sight, then he turned to Palfrey and said:

"So she has a kind of resistance to it."

"Either that, or the mosquito which bit her wasn't infected."

"Could be either. We want to find out."

Palfrey asked, deliberately obtuse: "Why?"

Matt said without a pause: "If she's built up a resistance against the poison, others may have done the same. We want to find them. We want to know how the resistance developed. We——" he broke off, and then brushed his hand agitatedly over his hair. "You know as well as I do."

"I know," Palfrey agreed. "We can't be positive that it was the carrier mosquito, though, as we've no proof that any were as near." He turned to the big map on the table by his side. "Here's the road you came along." He indicated it with his forefinger, and traced it slowly. "You say you met the girl about here, three miles from the spot where you turned off?"

"About three."

"Here are cottages," Palfrey said, and pointed to little dots, some distance off the road. "There's a small experimental farm in a clearing in the forest here too, all about the same place, but there's no response to telephone calls." He sat down and picked up a receiver, and spoke almost immediately. "Reggie? . . . Is there any report from any of the people believed to be in Area 23?" The map was divided into squares, each with a number, and the spot where Matt had met Kathleen O'Shea was inside that square. "Any response to telephone calls, or any reports of a visit? . . . Yes, ring me back as soon as you can." He rang off, and saw an odd little smile at Matt Stone's lips. "Now what's on your mind?"

"You've got it organized down to the last detail," Matt said. "I hand it to you."

"We've known this as a suspect area for some time, and we've been preparing plans for a yard by yard search to try to trace Rondivallo," Palfrey told him. "So we were ready for it. We're always terrified that some lunatic will unleash a bacteriological attack. One chemist plus one laboratory could kill millions. Our job is to be ready to act if the need arises." He changed the subject abruptly: "Think you scared the wits out of this girl?"

"It looked like it."

"If it proves that she has a resistance to infection, we have to find how she developed it," Palfrey said. "It could be a natural resistance, like some people's to ordinary mosquito bites, but I needn't waste words. You'd better talk to her. She'll soon know what's happening, and will know you weren't lying to her. That should have softened her mood."

"I can try," Matt conceded.

"Fine," said Palfrey briskly. "If I were you, I'd get dressed." He broke off when the telephone bell rang, and again picked up the receiver very quickly. "Yes?" He listened; and he was so affected that his knuckles showed white where he gripped the instrument. "All right Reggie, thanks," he went on. "Yes, Mitchison's on the spot, let me know if that fungi on the larynx shows again."

He rang off.

He could see Matt Stone's tension, and guessed that his own manner caused it; it was affecting all of them in much the same way. He smoothed down the silky hair at his forehead, and then said quietly:

"Seven people in Area 23, three of them within half a mile of the road you were on, have collapsed with all the usual symptoms, so those mosquitoes were the plague

126

carriers all right. And there's another thing you don't know yet."

"Yes?"

"Larsen is back. He walked and rode through part of the area and wasn't touched," Palfrey said. He tried to judge Matt's reaction, and after a pause he went on: "You didn't take to Larsen, did you?"

"I wouldn't have taken a liking to any man under those conditions," Matt said. "I've been arguing about it with myself. If I'd been in his position, maybe I would have done the same thing. It must have looked as if I was trying to ravish the girl."

Palfrey thought: "He's got a quality of honesty that doesn't come often, honesty with himself. And they don't come with more guts."

But Matt Stone had come through the infected area unhurt.

There was another thing. He had been in it for hours, had walked about, moved in the open not once but several times, and had not been bitten; or if he had been bitten, had not suffered. That was a fact which could not be ignored. Stefan Andromovitch and any of the other leaders of Z5 would be quick to seize upon it. Other people in cars had been infected; Matt hadn't. And although he'd used the insecticide at times, at others he hadn't.

Andromovitch would say: "We must be very careful with him, Sap." A man could serve Z5 for years and then betray it; loyalty had to be tested time and time again.

Matt said: "What do you want me to do right now?"

"Order some tea in your room," Palfrey said promptly. "I'll arrange for Kathleen O'Shea to bring it. Talk to her, and see what you can find out."

Matt said slowly: "Fair enough. Thanks. If you know my room number, I'll go along."

"Twenty-eight," Palfrey said, and saw him to the door,

127

and then turned back into the room. The knuckly Sarak, who was no more than five feet six in height, was taking a telephone message. When he put the receiver down, he spoke in his careful, heavily-accented English:

"There iss von child, a girl, in Area 31, not hurt."

"Is she being taken to Lauriston?"

"Yes."

"Mitchison is there," Palfrey remarked. "He'd better be warned to be ready for her." He stood by the window, staring across the forest, then glanced at the map and saw the little redheaded pins, indicating places where people had been bitten and had collapsed.

As far as they knew, just four people had come through without hurt: Kathleen O'Shea, Larsen, this girl child, and Matt Stone.

He sat down and telephoned Lauriston Hospital. Mitchison came on the line at once.

"Hallo, Palfrey, I wanted a word with you. Several of the latest victims have the fungi infection of the larynx, and we're trying to isolate it. There are indications of similar infections in the gums, too. I should say that the trouble is infectious—through the mouth."

"The dust," Palfrey said, in a taut voice. "Have you had any samples of dust?"

"Yes. We've found that the larger insect discharges it," Mitchison said. "The insect isn't a true mosquito, by the way, we haven't yet identified it. We're checking sputum and the fungi from the larynx of infected people with the so-called dust."

"Living organism, that dust?"

"Oh yes," said Mitchison.

"Oh, God."

"I'll call you when there's any development," Mitchison promised.

Palfrey rang off.

He was ashen pale and his hands trembled a little.

He needed every man he could use, but dare he use Matt Stone any longer?

He spent ten minutes at the desk, going through reports, checking everything that had been done, satisfied that nothing could have been more swift or effective in this area. The civil and military authorities had sprung into action, and that in itself was reassuring, but they knew practically nothing yet. Even the precautions at the other centres where Rondivallo had been and where Z5 men had collapsed, and were now dead, might be pointless: there was no proof that widespread danger existed in any of those places.

The only indication here had been the murder of Dr Korven after the stroke which Mrs Hill had suffered. Korven and then Dimmock, and next the Carters, had all been killed after they had seen Mrs Hill, and possibly because they had seen her immediately after the seizure.

Was that the reason?

Three of the Z5 agents were at the cottage, which had been thoroughly decontaminated. Reports should soon be in. There were probably isolated spots in the forest where the paralytic insects were still alive, but the spray used would almost certainly kill all the mosquitoes which flew from the breeding ponds for the next twenty-four hours. After that, another spray from air would be necessary. It wasn't absolutely certain that the mosquitoes were carriers for the satellite dust, but it seemed likely.

Surely the research men working on the specimens would get results soon.

If not, and if the plague spread . . .

That was the fear which haunted Palfrey.

It was on his mind every waking minute, driving out every other thought, and he was trying to cope when the telephone connected with Andromovitch in London came through.

"Hallo, Stefan," he said, and pictured the Russian giant sitting at the huge desk. "Anything fresh?"

"There has been a plague of mosquitoes and satellites

in Buenos Aires," Andromovitch said. "A section of one of the suburbs is badly stricken, nearly everyone in it is paralysed."

Palfrey felt coldness spreading through him as the meaning of this struck home.

Here, in this peaceful English village, there was the horror of the plague.

Five thousand miles away the same plague was ravaging the people, the young and old together, the helpless and the innocent.

"Anywhere else?" Palfrey made himself ask.

"Yes," the Russian said. "There is a warning from the British Government that Matthew Stone is a bad security risk. I have asked for details but none are forthcoming."

Palfrey asked very softly: "Did anyone in particular name Matt?"

"I had an official memo, signed by the Prime Minister's secretary. That is all I know," Stefan said.

Matt went into his own room for the first time since arriving at the hotel. It was at a corner, and overlooked the rolling countryside as much as the forest. He saw a road winding over a hill, and, at the highest spot, a great oak tree; that was the look-out point where he had stood with Yvonne, who had been so aloof and cold, and yet now seemed to obsess him because the mark of death was on her.

He found his two suitcases in the room, his clothes unpacked; was that hotel service or done by Z5? He changed slowly, hanging the bathrobe in his own bathroom. He felt much less tired and harassed, but there had been something in Palfrey's manner which he hadn't really understood, or greatly liked.

He went to the large single bed, walking on thick yielding carpet. The hotel was the height of luxury; all the furnishings and the fittings were good, the décor was excellent; it was a kind of millionaire's home from home. He lifted the telephone, and asked for tea, and remembered being served by the grey-haired woman at Palfrey's office yesterday—a thousand years ago. He lit a cigarette and stood by the window, looking for tiny dots representing houses and buildings. On a road a long way off he thought he saw a string of moving cars.

What was in Palfrey's mind?

How far could the plague spread?

How had the girl Kathleen O'Shea escaped without harm?

He heard a tap at the door, called come in, and turned round slowly, the cigarette at his lips. The maid had a small white cap on her beautiful coppery hair, carried the tray easily, had a bearing which reminded him of women of the East. It was not until she was halfway towards the table in the window that she recognized him. The cup and saucer chinked as she stopped abruptly.

Matt said: "Hallo, there. Remember me?"

"Yes, I remember you," she said, with that touch of Irish brogue. "Only too well, sir."

"Have you heard what's been happening?"

"Indeed I have, and a terrible thing it is." She put the tray down, and glanced at her arm, covered now by a black silk dress; the curves of her figure was hinted at by the absurd little white lace apron. "When I heard that what you said was really true it was a panic I was in, and you were to blame for it!"

"But you're all right?"

"Except that I'm badly worried," she said. "Perhaps there could be delayed action, sir. But there's been a doctor to examine me, and he says that the bite on my arm is an ordinary mosquito. I didn't think the time would ever come when I was grateful to a mosquito, but there it is. Will that be all?"

"Do mosquitoes usually bite you badly?" Matt asked.

"Sure they do, and I have my share of them."

"Have you taken anything to stop them from poison-

131

ing you, and making sure the bites don't swell up too much?"

"I've never had to take a medicine against mosquito bites," she scoffed. "There was a big water scare here only a few weeks ago, sir, and all of the staff had to take medicine to make sure it didn't upset them, but to be sure no one said anything about mosquitoes." She paused, and Matt tried to make sure he couldn't see the effect her words had on him, could not guess at the way his heart began to race. "I'm not sure now—is it you who should apologize to me, or do I owe myself an apology?" Her eyes were glowing.

In spite of the situation, Matt laughed.

"I'll apologise," he said, and went on quietly, laughter soon dying: "I thought you would be paralysed in the next few minutes. Are you sure that you've never taken anything to help you from the ill effects of mosquito bites?"

"I've told you already," she said, and looked round at the door. "I can't stand here any longer talking to you, sir, Mrs Larsen will want to know if I'm trying to flirt with one of the guests. I wouldn't be the first girl to be sent away with a flea in her ear, and I can't say that I blame her."

Mrs Larsen, Matt thought; not the manager himself.

"Who else was sent away for that?"

"I should know if anyone does, it was my own sister," Kathleen said. "She came here from County Down to get the job, and pleased indeed she was with it. Do you know she was sending home to mother and father ten pounds a month, and said she was living easy even after that? And then she took up with a guest at the hotel, and didn't hold the job much longer."

"Who was the guest?" Matt tried to sound only casually interested.

"It's very curious you are, and if it's information you want why don't you ask Mr Larsen, unless you're frightened of him."

"Who was the guest, Kathleen?" asked Matt, all pretence gone.

He knew that, standing there against the window, he looked as attractive to a woman as he was ever likely to be; and he had no sense of false modesty. He was young and good-looking, and there was the glint in his eyes and the little smile at his lips, all calculated to set her heart a flutter, and if the way she looked at him was any guide, he was succeeding. Her honey-coloured eyes were beautiful with the glow of excitement, and she did not seem frightened of what was happening all around them.

Matt thought: "My God, she's really lovely."

She spoke swiftly.

"It was an Australian, which is more than any American can say for himself! And what would I be doing divulging private information to a stranger?"

"Was it Mr Rondivallo?"

The girl caught her breath.

Matt could not be sure, but believed that Rondivallo meant much more to her than the name of the man who had disappeared with her sister. She was startled, almost shocked, by the fact that he knew who it was. Talk of the mosquitoes, of the paralysis, of the disaster, could not shock her, and that was easy to understand: for she had been immune and had not looked upon the victims. But the name of Rondivallo shook her badly.

"I wasn't here when it happened and I didn't know his name," she said hastily, and turned on her heel. "You'd best be drinking your tea while it's hot." Before he could stop her, she reached the door, and looked over her shoulder swiftly.

Afraid?

"Don't go, Kathleen," he said, and drawled her name and liked the sound of it and the look of her. "Come and see if this was the man." He took the photographs out of his pocket.

"How could I tell you if I'd never set eyes on him?"

she demanded, and opened the door. But she didn't go into the passage: she gasped and backed into the room again. Beyond her Matt saw the little chunky European, Sarak, who followed her in, closed the door behind her. For the first time, Matt looked hard into the European's face. He saw the grimness in his expression and wondered what deep secrets lay behind his narrowed, pale grey eyes.

"*He* says that we must make her tell us what does she know about Rondivallo," Sarak said quietly, and "he" could only mean Palfrey. He stood looking up into the girl's face, his own set and stern, and she stared in a kind of desperation at Matt.

"Will you make him let me pass that door?" Anger merged with the alarm in her voice.

"You can go just as soon as you've told us all you can about Rondivallo," Matt said, "and all you can tell us about your sister, also. Did she know Rondivallo before she came here?"

"She did not."

"Was she a servant here when he came?"

"Yes, sure and she was."

"Did you know anything about the affair she was having with him when you were in Ireand?"

"No, and there's no call to keep asking the same question!"

"Kathleen," said Matt very quietly, "we're here to try to find Rondivallo, because he might know the cause of the plague." He waited just long enough to let that sink in, and it seemed to shock her more than anything else had done. He could actually see the blood draining out of her cheeks; her eyes seemed to burn bright because of it, and her lips were scarlet against her pallor. "We must find Rondivallo. He was here with your sister for some weeks, then both of them disappeared. Do you know where they went?"

"No," Kathleen said in a gasping voice. "As true as I'm

134

standing here, I don't know a thing about it. Is it true you think that Rondivallo might be able to stop——" she couldn't finish.

"Yes, it is," Matt said. "Why did you come here, Kathleen?"

"Isn't it obvious why I came?" Kathleen said huskily. "Maureen was missing, and we didn't hear from her at all in three whole weeks, and all of us were worried to our graves. So I came to find out if I could help her. The solemn truth is that we thought she'd found herself in trouble, and if that was so we wanted to help her, we didn't want her to be alone in England perhaps deserted by the man. Och, we may be Irish but we aren't fools, and we had wondered how it was she was able to send home so much money each month. 'Kathleen,' my father told me, 'there's a man with her, be sure of that, it's yourself who must go to England and find out all about it.' So I came, and Mrs Larsen gave me a position, and the wages are good. I can send home just as much as Maureen did, and there's no man helping me."

There was a little colour back in her cheeks now, and towards the end of the story her voice had become stronger. She glanced at the door, as if hoping she would be able to leave, but she did not ask if she could go. She would be missed, of course, the kitchen staff would know where she had come, and anyone in charge would probably wonder why she had been so long.

"All right, Kathleen," Matt said, and smiled at her again. "Did you look for Maureen when you came here."

She didn't answer.

"Did you try to find out where she'd gone, and where Rondivallo had gone?"

"No!" she cried. "There isn't a thing I can tell you about it." She turned swiftly towards the door and pushed past Sarak and turned the handle; but the door was locked, although neither of them had seen the man lock it. He did not try to bring her back, but stood

135

watching. She swung round with her back to the door and something near terror in her eyes. "It's as true as I'm standing here, there's nothing I know, nothing!"

There was something she knew and was afraid to tell. That much seemed certain.

How far should he try to drive her, now?

At any other time he would have let her go and planned to talk to her again, but hours—even one hour —could be of vital importance, and whatever it was she knew might be as vital. He needed time, to try to lull her fears; but was there time?

Then there came a sharp tap at the door. Matt was startled and Sarak looked round quickly, while Kathleen O'Shea cried:

"Who's there? Will you come and let me out?"

There was a moment's pause; in it, Sarak moved swiftly to one side, putting his right hand at his pocket, while the girl stood between Matt and the door. There was a sharp metallic sound, the handle turned and the door was thrust open.

Matt saw Larsen for the second time.

14. Larsen

LARSEN was strikingly handsome, and he came in with something of a swagger, and a glitter in his eyes. He had a horsewhip in his right hand, held straight down by the side of his leg, the lash curled round his fingers. He did not see the chunky Sarak as he closed the door, and let the end of the lash fall to the floor.

"What you want is a horsewhipping," he said. "That is what you are going to get. Move away, Kathleen."

"Mr Larsen, please, he meant me no harm! I swear it!"

"Move aside," Larsen said softly.

Kathleen moved to one side, while Sarak stood absolutely still, as if he intended to leave this situation to Matt. Matt looked into Larsen's handsome, coldly angry face, into eyes which were as pale a grey as Sarak's, and expected the first blow to come swiftly. He didn't move and didn't speak.

"Mr Larsen, sir, I swear to you he meant me no harm! What's a little kiss and a cuddle between a man and a maid? Don't do anything you'll regret, sir." The brogue was much more noticeable now, and Kathleen stretched out her hands in appeal.

Larsen behaved as if he hadn't even heard her.

"I'm going to teach you that American dollars don't buy the chastity of my staff," he said. "And I'm going to teach you that it doesn't pay to lay your hands on me."

His right arm moved, the whip hissed upwards.

"No!" gasped Kathleen.

Matt was smiling as if he had nothing at all to fear. As the whip rose he moved forward with a speed that took Larsen completely by surprise. He thrust his left arm upwards and caught the stocky part of the whip between the V of his thumb and forefinger, then gripped and twisted; and the whip seemed to tear out of Larsen's hand. It fell into Matt's, and he cracked it in bewildering succession, each time so close to Larsen's head that had he moved the manager would have been hit. But he stood absolutely still, ashen-faced.

Matt tossed the whip on to the bed, and the thin end of the lash trailed on the floor.

"There was one thing you didn't know," he said. "I was born in Arizona cattle country." His smile had never been broader, nor his voice quieter. "In my country we prefer to be friendly, Larsen, and if a man likes a girl, he says so. I like Kathleen, and I'm going to keep on telling her so. I don't know that I like you though. I haven't decided whether you're a big-head or a latter-day King Arthur. Did you use a pass-key to get in here?"

Larsen said thinly: "Yes."

"Next time you want to use it, give your guest time to open the door after your knock," said Matt. "If you don't, and it happens to be me, you'll get badly hurt."

"It won't be you," Larsen said, and his fury almost choked him. "You'll be out of this hotel in the next half hour, or I'll have you thrown out. Leave this room, Kathleen, and don't come back here. Don't speak to this man again while you are on my staff. If you do, you will be instantly dismissed. Do you understand me?"

"Yes, sir, indeed I do," Kathleen said humbly. She was already at the door, and opened it and hurried out, a frightened beauty.

"You heard me," Larsen said. "Pack your clothes and get out."

Again the door opened, very quietly. Matt saw it opening, but Larsen could not, for his back was towards it. Palfrey stepped in. He was smiling faintly, his slight stoop made him look shorter than he was, and inches shorter than Larsen. The immediate contrast was startling, although each man was fair. Larsen was so big and broad and massive, and by comparison Palfrey looked puny.

"Hallo, everyone," he said mildly, and Larsen spun round. "Ah, Mr Larsen. I'm sorry, but Mr Stone won't be able to leave yet. There's a state of emergency in this district, and you're under a kind of martial law. You won't notice it, except that you'll have to put up with some people you don't like."

"If I had my way, I'd send the lot of you packing!"

"Oh, no doubt," said Palfrey, in his mild, apparently ineffectual way, "but on this you can't have your own way, no matter how much right you have on your side. However, I will give an undertaking that none of my men shall worry your regular guests or the staff."

"If this swine worries Kathleen again, I'll break his neck," Larsen rasped. He turned, pushed past Palfrey, and stalked out.

As the door closed, Matt said: "Sap, I'm sorry. I handled that real badly."

"Could be," agreed Palfrey; "but, on the other hand, it could have been brilliant by mistake. No need to worry, anyhow." He was oddly impersonal. "Sarak, will you make sure that Larsen is watched, and tell Elise to keep a special eye on Kathleen O'Shea?" He waited until the knuckly European had gone out, then took out a packet of cigarettes and shook some out, and offered them to Matt. "The obvious thing first: is Larsen so interested in Kathleen because she's on his staff, because she's Kathleen O'Shea or because he hates your guts? We've had a man here for some time; one of the gardeners. He saw Larsen ride out after the girl this afternoon—he went on horseback and kept on the bridle paths, but he must have gone in the same direction as she did, or he wouldn't have been so near when you met her. Also, he rode through the forest where a dozen people were struck down by the plague, and wasn't affected. Incidentally, no animals are affected, only humans. Peculiar. Then he made it his job to find out where she was when she'd got back, and came to defend her honour." Palfrey drew deeply at a cigarette and smiled faintly. "Nice act. Did you learn anything from her?"

"Nothing really fresh," Matt said. He explained briefly, and went on: "If I learned anything, it's that she was too frightened to talk about Rondivallo."

"Yes," Palfrey said. "Matt, you seemed to have a way with Kathleen. Right?"

"It wouldn't surprise me."

"I'm going to try to arrange for you to spend some time with her soon," said Palfrey in that mild voice. "Before that, how do you see things now?"

"Do you mean, see things here at the hotel?"

139

"Yes."

"Like you, I simply guess," said Matt, and moved across to a large armchair and sat on the arm; he did not once look out of the window, although he was very close to it. "Kathleen's scared of Larsen, and Larsen wants to make sure that she doesn't tell me anything—presumably about Rondivallo." He didn't get up, but there was a new, urgent note in his voice: "Sap, don't take chances with that girl."

"I won't take unnecessary chances at all," Palfrey assured him. "Since we moved in, just before you arrived, we've stationed agents everywhere, including two in the kitchen and one on each of the bedroom floors. You're right, though, we have to make sure, so we have to take some kind of chance."

Matt said abruptly: "What kind?"

"We have to give Larsen time to try to get Kathleen away from here."

"You mean, give him time to try to kill her."

"He won't have a chance, she'll be too closely watched."

"I think he might take a chance," insisted Matt. "If he is working with Rondivallo on this hell's business, killing one girl more or less won't make the slightest difference to him. Why take the chance?"

"Because at the moment we're only guessing at Larsen's motives, and if it's possible we want to be sure," Palfrey said. "We want to break him down, and he's more likely to break if we can face him with evidence to prove that we know he's involved." He paused, while Matt knew that his own face was set and unrelenting, almost hostile because Palfrey was prepared to take this risk with the girl. And Palfrey's voice grew quieter. "If we had more time, I'd let you talk to Kathleen first and if that failed, try it my way. But we haven't enough time. Do you know what's happening in the world at this moment?"

Was that just a rhetorical question?

It seemed to burn into Matt's mind; like Palfrey's eyes, which seemed to change in front of him, and like Palfrey's expression, which showed a different man, a man of great strength and determination, and yet one possessed of a great fear.

Matt made himself ask: "Well, what is happening?"

Palfrey said: "There will be another news bulletin in five minutes, they are being broadcast hourly." He turned towards the window and looked out, while Matt said roughly:

"Do I have to wait for that?"

"I think so," Palfrey said, and didn't look round. "Let me tell you a little more. We don't know anything at all except that Rondivallo has disappeared, and that all of the outbreaks of this plague have taken place in districts which he has visited. You know what I told you before: now we know beyond all reasonable doubt that in Rondivallo's wake there is spreading horror and stricken multitudes. The village was only the beginning."

Matt said chokily: "But—but why?" He had a strange feeling that Palfrey was looking at him in a different way, was colder, was almost hostile.

"All we know is that the plague is following the trail of Rondivallo, and that this was the last place in which Rondivallo was seen," Palfrey said thinly. "We're waiting just long enough to try to get Larsen to make a false move. If he hasn't done that within the next hour, we'll start questioning every man and woman on the staff, every conceivable suspect. We've got to make them talk. Understand? Whatever methods we use, whatever pain we have to cause, we have to make them talk."

He moved to the radio set built into the wall and switched on; immediately a woman's voice sounded, with a background of swing music. Then a man's voice came, the familiar tone of a BBC announcer, touched perhaps with greater solemnity than usual.

. . . emergency news bulletin which should be re-broadcast throughout Europe, Asia, and any other parts

141

of the world where no similar announcement is being made. The Government regrets to have to announce that a plague of insects, some not unlike mosquitoes to look at but accompanied by a swarm of tiny satellites, something like a small cloud of dust, has descended upon certain parts of Great Britain, France, Hungary, Argentina, the U.S.A., Aden and Egypt. The infection carried by these swarms causes almost immediate signs of paralysis, particularly of the throat and larynx, which also show some of the signs of œdema of the glottis. Medical practitioners are advised that more detailed instructions for treatment will be given at the end of this bulletin. Meanwhile, for emergency use, household insecticides appear to have temporary stunning effect on the insects, which recover after a short while.

All local authorities throughout Great Britain are putting in hand special emergency arrangements to meet the possibility that the swarms might invade their district. All Civil Defence workers are instructed to report for duty at once, although it must be emphasized that there is no question of enemy action."

Palfrey's face was like stone.

"Isn't there?" Matt asked, and he felt choked. "Sap, is that the truth? Is there no question of enemy action?"

Palfrey said: "I don't know."

Matt had a strange feeling that Palfrey wanted to add: "Do you?"

Kathleen O'Shea went hurrying along the passage to the service stairs, looking behind her as if she was frightened of her own shadow; or frightened that a door might open and someone pounce on her. She reached the foot of the stairs and stood for a moment looking along the wide passages to the pantry where she prepared the afternoon teas, and where she knew that Larsen or his wife might be, or one of the other maids.

She went into the pantry.

No one else was there.

She stood against the sink for a minute or more, staring blankly ahead, and anyone who saw her must have known that she was terrified.

She went into the kitchen.

Here, five of the staff were preparing vegetables and pastry and meats for the evening meal, including the head chef, a short man wearing a tall chef's hat and completely enshrouded in white. No one appeared to take any notice of her, except one of the new kitchen hands, who had been taken on only that day; he kept glancing at her. There was obvious tension in everyone: an edginess which she couldn't fail to see.

She felt better now that she was with the others, and could watch the tea pantry and see if the call system, which glowed instead of buzzed, went on. It wasn't likely now, for few people would want tea so late. The cocktail bar would be busy and the wine waiters serving drinks in the lounges.

Then Larsen came in.

He was still white and his eyes had a glassy look. He saw her and stared intently; she wished she had been in the pantry, anywhere but here. He came towards her, and she did not notice that the new kitchen hand was watching them, and paying no attention at all to his work.

Close to her, Larsen asked in a low-pitched voice: "Did you tell the American anything?"

"No, sir, I didn't say a word, I swear I didn't, but he knew more than I thought anyone knew. I didn't utter a word out of place, sir, I did just what you always told me to do."

Larsen said: "If you say a word, your sister won't have a chance to live. Do you understand that?"

143

"Sure and I do, sir."

Larsen said: "Isn't it time you went off duty?"

"Well, sir, I suppose it is, I'd forgotten the time."

"It's half past six."

"Then I should have been off duty half an hour ago," she said. "What am I thinking of? I'll be going to my room!" She pushed past him, towards the doorway which led to the staff quarters, while everyone except the new kitchen hand was fussily busy, tins were clattering, gas was hissing.

Larsen followed Kathleen.

Scared eyes watched him go.

Palfrey was told of this on the telephone, for the hotel switchboard was now operated by a Z5 member.

"She'll be all right," Palfrey said. "He won't be able to go into her room without being seen. How is she?"

"Frightened out of her wits, I'd say."

Palfrey said, tight-lipped: "Rather like me. Thanks." He rang off, and looked down at the desk which was littered with notes, some in his own hand, some in Sarak's, all bearing the same tidings: of fresh outbreaks. Sitting here, with the evening light over the forest and no hint of the disaster in sight, it was hard to believe that it was really happening, that this wasn't a nightmare of facts and figures and dark menace.

A telephone bell rang, and he lifted the receiver.

"Hallo. Stefan?"

"Sap, an emergency meeting of the cabinet is being held tonight and you are asked to be at hand. A meeting of the International Red Cross is to be held in Geneva tomorrow morning, to organize relief work, and of the General Assembly of the United Nations tomorrow at noon."

Palfrey said: "Well, at least they're taking it seriously."

"Have you traced anything?" the Russian asked.

"We've men out in the forest and combing the countryside," Palfrey answered slowly, "but except for one or two people in the hotel no one whom we know saw Rondivallo down here can talk. That's the worst of it. They can't say a word. There's nothing from Mitchison yet. I'm giving Matt Stone plenty of rope, but will have to work on him if we don't get a move soon." His hand was at his forehead. "Stefan——"

"Every minute I am being harassed for reports," Stefan said. "Moscow telephoned twenty minutes ago, for the third time."

"Is there an outbreak there?" Palfrey's voice rose.

"There are two—one in the Ukraine, another near the Latvian border," Stefan's calmness seemed likely to crack. "There is a call on the way from Pekin also. Sap, no one has any kind of clue at all, the only hope is to find Rondivallo. For humanity's sake, can't you——"

"I'll tackle Larsen," Palfrey said abruptly.

"All right, Sap," Stefan said.

Palfrey turned away from the desk and went towards the door. The silent Sarak moved across to open it for him, and inclined his head, as servant to master. Palfrey went out. An agent was standing in sight, and raised his hand in salute. Palfrey passed with a nod, staring straight in front of him, and went down the wide staircase into the great hall. Two couples were sitting and drinking cocktails and eating potato crisps and nuts. Outside on the verandah was a young party, noisy with a false gaiety: and silence fell abruptly when another bulletin came over the air.

They had not been affected, except by the prevailing fear.

Palfrey turned towards the offices, past the reception desk, to a room marked *Private*. Opposite it stood another of the Z5 members, and Palfrey said:

"Is Larsen in here?"

"Been there for twenty minutes."

"By himself?"

"His wife's in there with him."

"Thanks," said Palfrey. He tapped at the door, and told himself that it was crazy, he should just turn the handle and go in. He hadn't adjusted himself to the desperate urgency, to the speed with which the situation had altered. And he was haunted by the possibility that Matt Stone was not reliable, might even be one of these people. He must be given a chance to betray himself. If he was tackled by straight questions and answers, he would deny everything. How could he be made to talk *soon*?

Palfrey turned the handle and pushed.

The door was locked and there was no reply.

He pushed again, and the middle-aged English Z5 agent came across.

"Any luck?"

"Sure they haven't been out?"

"Positive. They went in, drinks were taken in ten minutes afterwards, and that's that."

"Jameson at the window?"

"Yes."

"Go and check with him, will you?" Palfrey took a bunch of keys out of his pocket, including a master key which would open this door. He inserted it and twisted, felt the lock give, but could not open the door: so it was bolted. He put his shoulder against it, but it would take a giant to break down the heavy, solid oak. The quickest way would be to get in through the window. He moved after the other man, and saw him in a small paved courtyard, where standard roses were rich in reds and yellows and pinks. He was standing at the window and staring in.

Palfrey reached him.

Inside, Larsen lay in a peculiar position on a sofa, and his wife, a plump, pretty woman, sat back in an easy chair, her head lolling forward. Both were very still. Palfrey bent his elbow and cracked it against the window, and the other men helped to knock out the big splinters of glass.

146

Palfrey said: "Find Kathleen O'Shea," and then climbed into the room, which was high-ceilinged and pleasant, with a thick Persian-type carpet, and a small writing bureau in one corner, near the sofa. Whisky, gin, a syphon of soda, some glasses and other bottles stood there.

Neither of the Larsens moved.

Were they paralysed?

Palfrey reached them, and a moment later he knew that this wasn't the paralysis of the plague; they were both dead of poison.

"Find the waiter who brought their drinks," Palfrey said urgently.

"It was a girl," the English agent said.

"Recognise her again?"

"I should do."

"Go and try," Palfrey said urgently.

15. The One Voice

PALFREY moved swiftly and reached the hall where the receptionist smiled tautly and where the over-loud laughter of the four on the verandah came clearly. He went towards the domestic quarters. There was fear in him, lest the one voice which might be raised was silent too.

He passed a maid carrying some pillow cases.

He passed the chef, who looked as if he had just changed into a fresh white smock and a fresh white hat.

He reached the staff living quarters, and saw Jameson coming out of one of the rooms and another Z5 man standing just outside.

Palfrey said: "Is she——" and then stopped.

"She's okay," Jameson said. "She just seems struck dumb, that's all."

"*What?*"

"Oh, I don't mean——" Jameson said, and then Palfrey pushed past him and stepped into a small room, with two beds, a dressing-table, a corner wardrobe and two easy chairs. In one of these Kathleen O'Shea sat limply, her eyes open, her lips a little slack. She was alive, for she turned her eyes to look at Palfrey, although she gave no sign that she had recognised him. He felt the sweat at his forehead go cold and clammy, for he could not be sure; and these symptoms might mean that the girl had been poisoned too.

He stood in front of her: "Kathleen, listen to me. Have you had anything to eat or drink in the last hour or so?"

She shook her head.

"Sure? Nothing?"

She managed to say: "Nothing."

"Are you feeling ill?"

She shook her head again, then pressed her hands against her forehead and said:

"No, I'll be all right, be sure I will."

"What frightened you like this?"

She drew back. "I'm not frightened!"

"Kathleen, it is vitally important that you should tell me. What frightened you?"

"Nothing," she cried. "Nothing! I'm not frightened, I'm just tired, I'm not frightened."

"Did Larsen frighten you?"

She almost screamed: "No!"

"You needn't worry about him any more," Palfrey told her very quietly. "He's dead, Kathleen. There's no need at all to be frightened of Mr Larsen or his wife. Just tell me what happened."

"Nothing happened," she sobbed, and seemed worse now that she knew Larsen was dead; it had the opposite effect to that which Palfrey had hoped. "Go away from me! I'm tired, I want to rest, go away from me!"

In London, Stefan Andromovitch was saying to the Minister for Home Affairs:

"We are doing everything we can. The moment there is news, we shall tell you."

The Minister said: "If we can't stop it soon, by the morning there will be panic everywhere. We already know of seven outbreaks. Get Palfrey on the telephone at once. He must question Matthew Stone."

"Yes, I know," Palfrey said into the telephone. "It couldn't be any worse, sir. I'm getting reports from everywhere overseas, but so far there's been only one common factor, the paralysis following the mosquito bites, which seem accompanied by an infection of the larynx caused by breathing in the satellite dust."

"Palfrey, please don't tell me what I already know. Have you questioned Stone?"

"I shall shortly. When the Prime Minister's secretary said he was a bad risk, did it imply he's involved in this business?"

"I only know what Domminy told us," said the Minister. "He reported to the Cabinet that Washington warned him. He was on special duty, as Minister of Food and Agricultural Supplies. He asked Washington for details which aren't yet forthcoming. But we can't wait, you must tackle Stone."

"I need something with which to break him down," Palfrey said.

"Use *any* methods," the Minister urged.

It was like talking to a frightened child, and Palfrey could understand the reason for it. Crisis due to causes which men could understand might give rise to isolated panic; when the danger struck out of the blue and was absolutely inexplicable, when people could not safely walk in the street or open their windows without breathing in death, then panic could overwhelm a nation.

Palfrey switched on the radio, for another bulletin was due. Most of it was repetition, and he switched off as the telephone rang.

"Mr. Mitchison is on the line," a man said.

Ah!

"Put him through."

"Hallo, Palfrey," the specialist said in a tired voice which did not suggest he was in any way hopeful. "Haven't much for you. There's very slight radio-activity in the sputum, and also in the satellite dust, which appears to be a cluster of bacteria, several millions in one little cloud, of course. That's as far as we've got. I've told London, but no radio-active tests on the mosquitoes themselves or ponds where they breed have been positive."

"Any sign at all of a neutralising agent?" asked Palfrey.

"Not really. Miss Brown isn't too badly affected at the moment, and certainly isn't at death's door. We're analysing blood, sputum and other specimens to see if we can get a lead."

"Well, you can't do more," Palfrey said.

The long-distance telephone was buzzing, so he said goodbye, rang off, and picked up the other instrument.

There seemed no time to breathe.

"You again, Stefan?"

"Yes, Sap," said Andromovitch. "You must be told the worst news yet. A London theatre audience panicked when mosquitoes and the dust filled the theatre this evening."

Palfrey said: "So they've reached London," in a flat voice. "We'll have to forbid gathering in meeting-places of any kind."

"That is being done. There is another development, too. People are beginning to leave the country in any vessel they can find. Aeroplanes are being chartered privately, liners are being besieged. There are some ugly situations at the docks. At one port the police had to call on the military to restore order." Andromovitch was quiet voiced, almost relaxed, as if he had overcome the attack of nerves. "There is one good sign."

Palfrey asked abruptly: "Medical treatment?"

"Yes. Some cases have responded quickly to curare distillation injections, given subcutaneously." Stefan said. "One or two felt no effect after breathing in the dust. Your research establishments are working on it now, and supplies are being prepared, but it can never be enough for mass treatment."

Palfrey said: "Send me a supply, urgently," and put down the receiver and turned towards the door. It was nearly dark outside, but at last there was a glimmer of light in his mind. On the littered desk was a tray with a half-finished meal; nothing had stopped the staff from serving the food. There was no panic here, but a kind of unreal normalcy. How long would it last? This was an oasis of peace now, an oasis of security; but tight-lipped, nervous people were gathered round a radio as he went through the lounge towards the domestic quarters.

Matt Stone was outside Kathleen O'Shea's room.

"Matt," Palfrey said, as if everything was normal in his attitude to Matt," you've half an hour to make her tell you all that she knows. If she won't, we'll have to use harsh tactics. And don't tell me that you hate the idea."

"She stares at me as if she's really struck dumb," Matt said, "but I'll try again."

He tapped at the door, but there was no response. He opened it and stepped inside—and as he did so, he struck at something which flew into his face. Palfrey saw it: gnat or mosquito, or even fly, it made his heart turn over, and he stepped forward.

"She all right?"

"She's all right," Matt said. "Don't crowd us."

"Matt," Palfrey said, "I want you to take her up to your room. Get her out of these surroundings. They may be part of the trouble. Carry her, if needs be."

He saw Matt's head move up, abruptly, and then saw the American turned to stare at him. That appraisal seemed to last for a long time.

There was a microphone in Matt's room. If he said a word to the girl which implied that he was involved, it would be the weapon Palfrey needed.

Matt saw the expression in Palfrey's eyes, and sensed the nearness of absolute disaster. Hours had aged Palfrey as he had never seen a man age, and that showed more in his eyes than anywhere else. Matt saw more: Palfrey wanted him to take the girl upstairs because he didn't fully trust him. In that upstairs room there was the microphone link, and everything said could be overheard.

Well, why not?

Matt said: "Sure, I'll fix it," and turned to Kathleen.

She sat in the armchair where Palfrey had seen her, and had not moved since Matt had come in, twenty minutes ago. He had cajoled, pleaded, ordered her to talk, but she had said nothing that had mattered, although she had not lost her voice, for she had uttered odd words and had shown no signs of the paralysis. He could not tell whether she had heard Palfrey's instructions or not; certainly she made no attempt to get up.

"We're going upstairs to my room," he said. "You'll be more comfortable there."

"No," she said, chokily. "I will stay here."

"Kathleen, you're coming up to my room."

"I won't come, I want to stay here, I want you to go away!" she cried. "I don't know anything about Maureen, I don't know anything at all. Go away from me! I can't stand being questioned any longer, go away from me!"

Matt said: "We're going upstairs, Kathleen," and moved forward. She started to draw back, but he took her wrists, pulled her to her feet, and hoisted her over his shoulder. He held her so that she could kick and strike at his back, but could not get away. He turned towards the open door. He saw Palfrey and one of the other men just outside, and Palfrey formed words with his lips:

"Want any help?"

Matt shook his head, turned out of the room, and went towards the back staircase. With luck he would meet none of the staff or guests on the way. He did pass Z5 agents; he wondered how many of them were here now. The girl had stopped kicking, as if she realized that she was only wasting her effort. She was hardly a lightweight, and by the time he reached the door of his own room she felt very heavy.

Sarak stood outside, and he opened the door.

Matt carried the girl in.

He lowered her to an easy chair and backed away swiftly, half expecting her to spring towards the door. She just sat glaring, her lips wide open, breathing very hard. But it could not rob her of beauty; a kind of savage beauty now.

Matt knew what Palfrey feared.

He believed that the girl was very near the borderline of nervous collapse; that if she did collapse it would be impossible to make sure that she would talk. If he stepped up the pressure too much it would do more harm than good, and Palfrey realized it.

Palfrey didn't really trust him, and had to be convinced.

Matt pulled up a small chair, sat down in front of the girl, and took out cigarettes. He crossed to the radio, lighting a cigarette for himself, and switched on. Music flooded the room. He took the cigarettes to her and she accepted one: the first voluntary movement which she had made for a long time.

He lit it for her. The flame of the match seemed to burnish her eyes, and he was reminded of the eyes of a giant cat, tawny, shimmering.

"Like a drink?"

She shook her head.

"You ought to have one," he said. "You'll feel better after that."

The music stopped and a man said that the latest bulletin would be broadcast in half a minute. Matt stood smoking and looking down at Kathleen, seeing that she was not used to smoking and wasn't enjoying the cigarette. She had turned her head and was staring at the radio. She still wore the black dress, the white apron, the lace cap.

"..... this is the half-hourly emergency broadcast for the whole nation. The Government has issued a statement from Number 10 Downing Street, declaring a state of national emergency, but it is emphasized that the movements of the populace are a greater danger to the security of the realm and to the individual than the actual menace of the insects. Medical treatment in many cases is proving effective. The Government, however, has no desire to minimize the dangers inherent in the present situation, and a curfew has been imposed on the nation, to begin at nine-thirty this evening. This announcement will be repeated at the end of every bulletin. It is emphasized that householders should have insecticides handy, it now being fully established that most domestic and agricultural insecticides are fatal to the carrier insect, which closely resembles a mosquito.

"It is also generally known that . . ."

Matt switched off, and turned and said:

154

"Kathleen, whatever is keeping you quiet is nothing compared with what is happening outside. That bulletin gives you some idea, but only a glimmering. These insect swarms are killing thousands of people and paralysing hundreds of thousands more. Nothing matters against that." He made himself speak very slowly and didn't look away from her. "What is frightening you?"

She closed her eyes and her lips moved, and he just heard her say:

"They'll kill Maureen and they'll kill my parents. God curse them all their lives."

She seemed to have to fight to go on: as if the words tormented her.

"It was Larsen himself who told me what they'd do, and it's no comfort that Larsen is dead, he's not alone in all these evil things."

Matt asked softly: "Do you know who is working with him?"

"I don't know at all," she said. She opened her eyes and looked at him almost cunningly. "I don't know anything, except that I found out where Rondivallo had taken Maureen. But Larsen told me if ever I betrayed that——"

"He can't hurt you now," Matt said, and went to the telephone and lifted it and said: "Dr Palfrey, please." He waited only a second, while the girl stared at him. "Hallo, Dr Palfrey. Can you arrange for a special guard to be set on the home of Kathleen O'Shea, in Eire? . . . the town of Horan? . . . Yes, you have their address . . . Yes, telephone the request at once, please." He kept this voice formal and looked away from the girl; when he turned back, replacing the receiver, he saw a gleam which might have been of hope in her eyes. "It's all right," he said. "Within half an hour your home will be guarded by men who'll make sure nothing can go wrong, you needn't worry about that any more. Now will you tell me where Maureen went with Rondivallo?"

She said: "It is a place in the forest."

As she spoke, there was a distant booming sound, and then without warning the lights went out.

Kathleen cried: *"What's that?"* Matt heard her jump up and went swiftly to her side. She hadn't tried to make for the door, but was standing by the chair. He felt her foot against his as he groped, then he put an arm round her waist.

"It's an electrical failure, that's all," he said. "The lights will soon be on again. Where is this place in the forest?"

She didn't answer.

The first blackness had eased a little, and he could just make out the shape of her head and shoulders, and when he glanced round he saw the light of the stars, looking very bright. And there was another light, a yellow one, not more than a mile away; somewhere in the forest. It was a leaping light, too.

It shone on Kathleen's eyes.

"Never mind that," he said, and prayed that the lights would go on, to give her back brief courage. "This place in the forest, is it the agricultural experimental station?"

"Yes," she said in an empty voice. "Look, it is burning. And Maureen is there."

16.   Ring of Fire

HER words were whispered, as if she could not bear to utter them, and Matt could feel the stiffness of her body pressing against him as she stared towards the yellow light. She was right, for it was a burning light, the dance of flames which had started quickly and which now seemed to be leaping higher, and to be running to the right and to the left. Then he saw another burst of light in a more easterly direction: a third and a fourth.

The door opened.

He swung round.

The light of the stars had dimmed, but the light of the flames was fiercer now, and he could just make out Palfrey's figure in the doorway.

"You all right, Matt?"

"Yes."

"The lights will be on again in a moment," Palfrey said. "There's been a power failure, but I'm told there's an emergency plant in the hotel." He came nearer. "What has Kathleen told you?"

"Didn't you hear?"

"Everything electrical went dead," Palfrey said.

"Maureen is out there with Rondivallo," Kathleen said in that whispering voice. "In the forest." She moved towards the window slowly, and now the flames outside were so fierce that they spread a glow about the room, burnishing her features and turning her hair to a kind of fire.

Outside, the beams of torches were flashing and men were moving about. Suddenly, car lights were switched on and the whole of the front of the hotel was floodlit. Engines turned, and the headlamp beams carved strange arcs in the night as some of the cars were turned to face the steps and the lawns beyond, crisscrossing the whole of the approach to the hotel with light, some beams white and powerful, some much dimmer. Some of the cars were turned towards the sides, as if in defence formation.

The room light didn't come on.

Palfrey had come close to the girl.

"Do you know what part of the forest?"

"The agricultural experimental cottages," Matt said.

"It is in William's Glade," she declared slowly as if speaking really hurt her. "The farm."

Palfrey turned round. A light shot out from a torch in

his hand as he neared the door. He opened it and the light fell on Sarak's face.

"Get me the big map," Palfrey said.

Sarak turned at once.

Along the passage one of the hotel guests was saying: "It's outrageous, to plunge us into darkness like this. Something ought to be done about it."

"I don't suppose they could help it, dear," a woman said timidly.

"Then they damned well ought to be able to!"

Outside, the blaze in the forest was much fiercer, the flames were so bright that it was possible to see the smoke rising among them, and then towards the sky. Great patches of cloud seemed to cover the stars. The flames stretched a long way in each direction, and Matt could see that it was a ring of flames encircling a part of the forest. At first he thought that it was meant only to cut off the hotel, but other bursts of flame appeared and gradually he could make out a wide circle of fire without being able to guess its radius.

Palfrey spread the map out on a table and shone the torch on to it. As he traced the position of the glade, his pointing finger showed reddish white, the shadow sharp against the detailed map. Matt stood with his arm round Kathleen's waist, staring at the moving finger; and Kathleen looked deep into the flaming forest.

Palfrey's finger stopped.

"That's it," he said, and looked out of the window, "The fire is encircling William's Glade and the experimental farm. But we've searched it." He paused, then added roughly: "Bring her into my room." He went out, and Matt drew the girl towards the door; she strained against him, as if anxious to keep staring at the fire. Then she gave way, and he led her into the passage.

Lights came on, yellow and dull, but showing everything clearly enough; pictures on the panelled walls, two people at the head of the stairs, a maid carrying one lighted and a box of unlit candles, Palfrey striding towards his own room, and Sarak standing so that he could follow Matt. Sarak had not yet uttered a word.

Palfrey's door was open when Matt reached it, and the lights were on inside. The muffled throb of an engine sounded; so there was an emergency generator here, probably at one time there had been no grid electricity. Two or three other men were in the room, and all turned towards the doorway as Matt went in. The girl did not seem to notice them, just went towards the window, where the view was so beautiful by day.

Palfrey spoke into the telephone.

"Call the Lauriston and Winchester Fire Services by short wave, and call the two nearest military units for special fire-fighting equipment," he ordered crisply. "Arrange meeting places between here and the place where the fire is burning . . . The military units should be here within an hour." There was a note almost of hopelessness in his voice, but the tone strengthened as he went on: "What helicopters have we here? . . . Only the one? . . . All right, four of us can go, get it ready at once, will you? . . . Ten minutes, fine.

"What's that? . . . Larsen put in a call to Whitehall 96871, but there was no answer . . . just before we found him dead, was it? Ask London to try to trace that number." He seemed to add silently: "Any straw's better than none."

He rang off.

"Now, I want to know more about your sister being at William's Glade," he said to Kathleen. "Everything, at once."

She told him, now.

She had come here to find out all she could about Maureen, and had soon heard about Rondivallo, the big man who lived here. Maureen was known to have gone into the forest with him to help with some kind of agricultural research.

Kathleen had found her way to the glade, a clearing in the heart of the forest, with low, wooded hills behind

159

it, a stream, and some swampy land not far away. She had gone there on her bicycle one day, and wandered in the woods where Maureen had wandered, come upon the farm—and seen Maureen!

"She had a cottage, somewhere in the forest," Kathleen said in that shocked voice. "But she was taken away and I didn't see her again."

"Taken?" Palfrey interrupted.

"When I came back Mr Larsen told me so. And he told me that if ever I talked of seeing Maureen it was Maureen who would be killed. This very day he told me that if I spoke to anyone about this my parents would be killed, old though they are," she went on hoarsely. "What could I say to you?"

"Why did you go into the forest today?" Palfrey asked.

"I hoped to see Maureen." Kathleen said wearily. "I was near the glade when I met you, Mr Stone." Her voice was flat and unemotional, and the firelight still flickered on her eyes. "And after you'd gone Mr Larsen asked me why I was there; he wanted to know if I'd talked to anyone about Maureen. Of course I had not, for I dared not."

"You needn't be frightened any more," Palfrey assured her gently, and went on to Matt: "We want the cottages inside that ring of flames, and we need parachute forces in support." He looked at Matt. "You coming with the advance party?"

"You could wait for the parachute troops."

"We don't know how long they'll be. Hours, certainly. We can be there in ten minutes," Palfrey went on, moving towards the door. "If they've started that fire deliberately and it looks as if they have, then it might be to keep us away for a few hours. They'll know that we can break through the fire once we have the right equipment—some armoured cars could do it in half an hour. So we're in a hurry."

He was at the door.

"Sure, I'm coming," Matt said. He squeezed Kathleen's hand, then dropped her arm and turned and hurried after Palfrey. The light was still dim and yellow, but at least it revealed everything. Palfrey was talking over his shoulder, loudly and clearly; Matt couldn't understand it, could not see what was making him talk so that anyone could hear. Hotel residents, now in the main lounge, some at card tables, some still near the radio and television sets, heard every word as Palfrey elaborated the plans: how they would get inside the circle of flame and make sure that whatever Rondivallo set out to do could be stopped.

They went out.

Not far off, a helicopter engine was reverberating on the night air. The car headlamps were still on, showing many men moving about. Palfrey led the way towards the sound of the roaring engine. Soon it was so dark that he needed to show a torch on the gravel path. The roaring became louder, almost deafening. He stopped at a small cement outhouse, opened the door and ushered Matt inside. It was a gardener's shed, filled with tools, smelling strongly of creosote.

"Now what's on your mind?" Matt asked, and he tried not to be abrupt, tried to see Palfrey as the quiet, ruminative, but outstanding leader of Z5, a man of vision, of courage and of genius; not as a man who didn't trust him.

"We're not going to William's Glade just yet," Palfrey said quietly. "There could only be one reason for that ring of fire, to draw us into it. And they wouldn't want to draw us into it if they really wanted us there. I'd say that they guess that Kathleen's told us about the glade, so they expect us to be ready to move against it. That your guess, too?"

Matt leaned against the wall.

"You could be right. Where do we go from here?"

"We sent four men up in the helicopter, carrying shortwave radio, and they radioed reports telling us just what's on inside there," said Palfrey. "We'll get to work on the one thing that matters now—finding out who is behind this."

Then he added:

"Who is it, Matt?"

The air in the shed seemed to go cold. Matt didn't say a word, and Palfrey stared at him intently: coldly.

"Well, who?"

"Sap, it's been obvious that you've stopped trusting me," Matt said very slowly. "I'd like to know why."

"A Washington message to London said you were a bad risk."

"It's not true, Sap."

"I've got to assume it is until I can prove it isn't," Palfrey said. "You know what's on. You know that a life or two more or less won't really make much difference. Matt, look at some facts. You've been through the infected areas and haven't been hurt. Some other people seem to be immune too: the guests and the staff here. They knew Rondivallo, and you knew a lot about him. Where is he, Matt? What is he doing?"

Matt spoke very slowly:

"I don't know a thing, Sap. I'm on the level. Show me a way to prove it." There was a moment of chill silence. "Just show me a way. I hate all this as much as you do."

"Matt, I've got to know the truth," Palfrey said as if painfully. "I've got to find out if you're a Rondivallo man. I've got to bring pressure on you which I wouldn't want to use on anyone. I've got to make you talk."

Matt said: "How can I make you understand that it's all a waste of time?"

"You can hate me for it, you can blame me for it, but there's one way that I can make pretty sure that you're not one of them, Matt: that's by finding out if you're immune. You have to be put in an infected area. We've isolated some insects and their satellite swarms, and I have some in a small box. Here."

He took his hand out of his pocket, and showed a

small plastic box—match-box size. The light was good enough to show the mosquitoes and the little "cloud" inside it.

"If you're stricken after an attack, then I shall take it that you're cleared," said Palfrey. "If you're not—then I'm going to assume you are a Rondivallo man, and I'm going to make you talk. Any arguments?" Palfrey asked, still painfully.

"Just go ahead," Matt said.

Palfrey said: "I don't know what to hope for."

He opened the door with one hand, holding the small box in the other. A soft wind blew in. Matt did not see the other Z5 men outside, did not see Palfrey's expression, saw nothing but the little plastic box. Palfrey held it poised, and then tossed it against the wall. It struck and broke, and the mosquitoes flew out. Then Palfrey went outside and closed the door.

It was still light in here; light enough to see.

Matt stared at the broken pieces of the box, then heard the familiar, dreaded, humming sound. He saw the satellite clouds. He felt a cry rise to his lips. He wanted to shriek, to fling himself against the door, to do anything to save himself, but Palfrey might think he was putting on an act.

A mosquito settled on the back of his hand and he brushed it off; but immediately another settled on his forehead, and he felt its bite.

17. The Ordeal

MATT felt himself shudder as the tiny bite came, less painful than a pinprick; then he slapped his hand on his forehead and felt the mosquito squash. Slowly he drew his hand down and stared at it; there was the little splotch of blood. The fit of shuddering was uncontrollable. He leaned against a bench and let it have its way; and as she shivered he felt another tiny pain at his left hand. But that wasn't all. He felt as if his mouth was suddenly full of dust, was dry, was so dry that he couldn't speak.

God!

He couldn't *speak*. There was a lump in his throat, pain there too, like burning.

He hated Palfrey.

He hated Z5.

He felt sweat on his forehead as he moved, and was surprised to find that his muscles still served him. Would they, for long? The burning in his throat wasn't unbearable, rather like the beginning of a cold, but the burning sensation had come on so suddenly.

He felt a burning in his legs too, and then in his arms. He stared stupidly at his feet. This was it, then: the end. He wasn't immune, and Palfrey could be satisfied, Palfrey would probably send flowers to his funeral.

Damn Palfrey, damn Z5.

He tried to speak, but no sound came; he tried to shout, but now it was difficult even to move his lips. His legs were quivering and they felt weak, as if they would give way at any moment.

They were giving way!

Then he heard a sound, heard the door open, and a moment later saw Palfrey and another Z5 man.

"All right, Matt," Palfrey said, "you've had enough."

They had to carry him out.

They took him into the cool night air, and then Palfrey revealed a hypodermic syringe. He didn't speak as he injected a colourless liquid into Matt's forearm, but as he drew the needle out, he said:

"With luck, you'll be yourself again in half an hour."

That was a lie.

"We've found one counter-agent which works, but have very little of it," Palfrey said. "It's being used on volunteer guinea-pigs, to help our research men follow

164

the signs from the moment of infection. You'll be all right, Matt. Rest here, and I'll be back as soon as I can."

At least he was no longer suspect.

Palfrey walked from the hut in the garden briskly, but his shoulders were rounded and he seemed to be studying the ground. As he reached the main hall, the man who had been complaining about the lights came hurrying forward with a hand outstretched.

"Here, you," he said abruptly.

Palfrey looked up, into a fat face, at a bulky man, who was probably in his middle forties. The gourmet type. His eyes looked angry and his voice held a touch of anger too.

"Me?" asked Palfrey mildly.

"Yes, you. I'm told you're in charge of the hotel in the absence of Mr Larsen. Tell your men to let me go out, at once."

"Ah," said Palfrey. "They won't let you, of course. It could be dangerous outside."

"Nonsense. I go out for a post-prandial every night, and I don't intend to change my habits. All this nonsense about a state of emergency is a lot of alarmist folly. Just tell your men to let me go out."

"Sorry," Palfrey said. "It wouldn't be wise." He turned to go and saw the other man move his right arm; so he wasn't surprised when a hand descended heavily on his shoulder.

"Don't come the high hat with me. I'm going out, or I'll know the reason why."

"The radio can tell you the reason why," Palfrey said.

"There are dozens of men in the grounds. If it's dangerous for me it's dangerous for them."

"Oh, indubitably," Palfrey agreed mildly. "But they're paid for it." He shrugged himself free and walked off.

The bulky man stood glaring. Other residents of the hotel were still in the lounge, most of them now staring at Palfrey, although some were looking out of the window, where it seemed as if the whole forest was on fire.

Palfrey went upstairs.

One of the Z5 men followed him, to make sure that no one attacked; and Sarak was standing just outside the door of the room he had taken over. Palfrey nodded to him as he opened the door. Three men sat at the big table, and one jumped up quickly; a wispy kind of man probably much older than he looked; he seemed to be in the middle twenties.

"Anything new in, George?" Palfrey asked.

"The Cabinet's in session. Stefan says that there'll be a stink if you don't get to London pronto. Not his own words, mind you." George's face had an earnest expression, and there was not a vestige of a smile. "I said you'd call him."

"Get him for me, will you?" asked Palfrey, and sat down in a chair which one of the other men pushed forward. George picked up a telephone. "Lull in reports of new outbreaks?"

The two sitting men nodded.

"Deaths?"

"About one out of four, so far."

Palfrey pulled a face. "Hell of a proportion," he said. "I hope to heaven that curare distillation works on Matt Stone."

"It has on everyone who's been injected with it within half an hour of the infection," the man said. He was a sleek, dark-haired forty, with a slight cast in one eye, immaculately dressed, and with a deep, impressive voice. "Getting at them quick enough is the problem."

"Wish it was the only one," Palfrey said bleakly. "Getting enough of the curare is going to be the main problem. Doubt if we could treat a thousand cases in this country, and there will be tens of thousands of victims by the morning." His voice was dry and unemo-

166

tional. "Get me some coffee and sandwiches, Phil."

"Right." The dark-haired man stood up.

"Having trouble getting Stefan?" Palfrey asked, and George nodded but didn't speak, and then said: "Here he is, he's in the Cabinet room at Number 10."

"Ah," said Palfrey. "Thanks."

18. The Ultimatum

STEFAN Andromovitch sat at a corner of the large oval table at Number 10, acutely aware of the fact that every Minister, from the Prime Minister downwards, was staring at him. He had never faced a meeting of such men as these on his own before; Palfrey had always been there as spokesman. It was one of the few occasions when Stefan felt that his nationality was a serious obstacle. None of these men had reason to like Russia or Russian policy, and it was difficult to break down the prejudice towards an individual. Men in Z5 could, but they had trained themselves to it.

He was waiting for Palfrey to come on the line.

The crowded room was silent. A haze of tobacco smoke filled it, and the predominant odour was of cigar tobacco. But for the tension in each man this would have been the most ordinary looking meeting. Each man wore a black coat, a grey tie, a stiff white collar. The formality of the English was part of their stubborn strength.

Then Palfrey said: "You there, Stefan?" and a loudspeaker carried his voice, on a muted tone, so that everyone in the room could hear it. The Minister for the Colonies, who was slightly deaf, used a hearing aid.

"Hallo, Sap," Stefan said, and immediately felt easier, for it was as if Palfrey was in the room. "You know that I am at a meeting of the Cabinet, don't you?"

"Yes. Sorry I couldn't make it," Palfrey said, quietly and clearly. "I think developments, when they come, will be down here in the Forest of Conne. I'm sure that this is one of the centres of the trouble, and have no doubt that there's some human directing force, little doubt that the situation is to be used as a kind of blackmail. If it weren't, it wouldn't have happened simultaneously in so many places. We've no idea of the location of the other main operational centres, such as we have here, so we have to wait for our chance."

"Have you worked on Stone?" Stefan asked.

"Yes. He's been infected and is recovering now. Certainly he wasn't immune, and I think anyone working on the other side would be. Have you had any further information from Washington?"

"No. Mr Domminy received the message," Stefan said. "Is there any hope at all of quick results?"

"I've reason to believe that some of the residents or the staff of this hotel might be involved, and I'm going to take them one by one. A number of them work at Wide World Foods, mostly on the managerial and executive side. Is Mr Domminy at the meeting, by the way?"

There was a stir as a small plumpish man, with a bald pate and bushy hair at the sides and back, glanced at the Prime Minister.

"Yes," said Stefan.

"As Minister of Food and Agricultural Supplies he is in constant touch with Wide World," Palfrey said. "Does he——"

"Know the directors very well indeed," Domminy interrupted. "They grow some of the finest, the very finest crops of all kinds, and their canning and deep-freeze plants are ahead of any known anywhere in the world. On my recommendation the Government subsidised their work."

"So I understand." Palfrey's voice sounded dry. "I ought to see them at once, Mr Prime Minister, and if Mr Domminy will tell me who he deals with there——"

168

"Oh, the managing director," the Minister said. "A great man who has dedicated himself to feeding the poor and hungry, a practical believer in feeding five thousand with the pitifully inadequate loaves and fishes. But why you should think that he might be able to help you."

"Thank you, sir," Palfrey broke in. "I'll see Mr Harrison about those members of his staff resident at the hotel. As you already know, the manager Larsen is dead—probably murdered with poison in his drink. You will have the general report of the position, the places where outbreaks have occurred, the number of casualties, the methods tried to arrest the advancement of the paralysis, the fact that so far curare is the one drug which has proved of any use. You've already reported the advice that members of the Government and others of similar importance to the State should have facilities for subcutaneous injection available all the time."

"Let me speak to Palfrey," the Prime Minister said, and picked up a telephone near him. "Palfrey, this is Meddon speaking. All leading scientists and doctors have the facilities, of course, but there isn't anything like enough to go round." Meddon spoke in a cut, clipped voice. "There are now seven places in this country where outbreaks have occurred and in some there is a state of panic. There is every reason to believe that similar situations might arise overseas; there are already reports of it from Western Europe. I want something much better than you've given us."

Half of the men round the table nodded, most of them vigorously.

Domminy said: "So I should think!"

"Mr Prime Minister," Palfrey said formally, "it is less than twelve hours since we were aware of the emergency."

"Ah." Meddon grunted. "Yes. But we need miracles."

"Is there any encouragement from abroad, sir?"

The Prime Minister said slowly: "There is no indication

of any kind from any source that any progress has been made towards finding the breeding grounds of the insects, or finding out who is controlling them. Palfrey——" there was a break in his voice.

"Yes, sir?"

"What do you consider are the possibilities that the causes of this are not traceable by normal methods?" The Prime Minister hesitated. "In other words, have you any indications at all that the sources of infection are from places beyond the earth's orbit?"

Stefan could imagine Palfrey smiling at this; and could also see the tension on the faces of the other men round the table. Only three seemed to reject the possibility out of hand.

Palfrey said mildly: "You mean from another planet, sir?"

"Yes."

"The simple truth is that I don't know," answered Palfrey, "but I think the source will be found on earth all right. In any case, our problem is whether we can control it. If the Forest of Conne is one of the main operation centres, then I think we have a chance." His voice sounded as if it were further away: "They're back from the forest?" There was another pause, and then he spoke more loudly again: "I've a reconnaissance party back from a job, sir. Shall I call you back?"

"We'll hold on." The Prime Minister sat with the receiver in his hand.

Stefan looked at one Minister after another; some old, some youthful, all wise in their own generation, all men of wide experience, men who had sat to discuss matters of awful import to both the nation and the world. He saw how most of them stared at the telephone, how they all seemed to be motionless—even Domminy, who had covered his face and was in an attitude of prayer, until one man took his cigar from his lips and said:

"Can't possibly concede the possibility of interplanetary action. Can't possibly."

The Prime Minister didn't speak.

"We don't know what conditions we are creating," a small, lean, pale-faced man said. His eyes were so sunken that he looked almost like a skeleton over which the skin had been stretched. "It may be that radio dust in particles so small they do not affect human beings are infecting and affecting a kind of mosquito. The breeding grounds may be everywhere. The rate of growth may have been speeded up. When we decided to take upon ourselves the responsibility of interfering with nature we——"

"Are you there, sir?" It was Palfrey, but there was no note of excitement in his voice; just flatness. "There was a fire in the forest, and it appears to have destroyed several small experimental forest clearance and farming stations which we examined without result this afternoon. There is some evidence of extensive research, some evidence of radio-activity in materials found there. Seven dead men were discovered tonight. We may have something to work on, but nothing to offer quick results."

The Prime Minister did not speak, and the stillness affected the others in the room, making it look as if they themselves had been paralysed.

Palfrey went on almost apologetically: "One thing is to distribute insecticides and deal with it as a state of emergency. Have all suspect districts sprayed immediately with the insecticides, and hope for the best."

The Prime Minister said: "Yes. Very well. Thank you." He rang off, and Stefan put the receiver down at the same moment. The Prime Minister's face was colourless and he looked tormented; anguished. "Yes," he repeated and licked his lips. He looked slowly round at the tableau at the table, and when he spoke his voice

171

sounded very faint. "There appears to be nothing at all we can do."

Domminy spoke in clear, ringing tones:

"It is the hand of God. It is a visitation upon us for our folly in defying the laws of God and of nature. It would be understandable if God were to wipe all of us out. It might be possible then to start afresh and to build a world free from such follies. Others before me have dreamed such a dream. But I do not go all the way with them. I believe that even at this late date it is possible to redeem not only peoples but nations. I am sure you all agree with me. There is no reason to believe that mankind is beyond salvation."

A man next to Stefan said under his breath: "Save us from this pious nonsense."

Another said: "Shhhh."

A third interrupted the little Minister. "We all respect your religious views, Domminy, but we are now faced with a material crisis."

"I don't see what good would come," began the Prime Minister, stirring himself, "unless you advocate a day of prayer. Hmm, yes. A day of prayer might at least help to reassure the people."

"My dear Prime Minister," said Domminy, "I have no intention of advocating a day of prayer. Such days have been held in the past and millions have paid lip-service. They have been frightened into praying, and directly the emergency has passed, have they changed their ways? They have not. Some material way has to be found to deal with a materialistic situation. The present position is that we, and the rest of the world, are faced with a plague which could wipe out mankind. We have evidence of it. We do not require *further* evidence, I am sure. This should be sufficient to frighten all of mankind into its senses. While some of the outbreaks have been extremely serious, most will prove to be minor, if we are wise. A shock paralysis, fear, followed by a tranquillizing agent, then recovery, with the dread of what

172

might follow if the plague should strike them again. *That* would keep people away from sin."

Domminy paused.

Stefan Andromovitch lifted the telephone very slowly, watching the little man intently.

This was the man who had passed on doubts about Matt Stone.

No one moved; everyone stared at Domminy with slow, awful comprehension. His lips and jaw worked like those of a ventriloquist's doll.

"What we are facing is a new kind of force, with which to compel the application of the moral and religious laws," Domminy went on. "I am authorized to inform you that the outbreaks of what it pleases some of you to call a plague can be stopped and will be stopped as soon as this Government and all Governments have accepted the one condition which will be laid down."

A man gasped: "My God!"

"There will be only one condition, gentlemen."

Stefan had the telephone at his ear. No one else looked away from the Minister, who paused as if for breath.

"Are you calling, sir?" an operator asked.

Stefan whispered: "Get me Dr Palfrey, at the Forest Hotel."

"Yes, sir."

"The one condition is very simple," continued Domminy who was sitting at the table with his hands clasped lightly in front of him. "That is the destruction of all weapons of offence and defence, beginning with the destruction of all atomic piles, which are said to be intended for peaceful purposes which can of course be turned at any time to the pursuit of war. The destruction of all military aircraft, of all vehicles and guns, all armed ships, all ammunition, all rockets, all guided missiles and all small arms. For decades men of goodwill and of intelligence had been endeavouring to persuade the world to settle all its disputes by discussion and peaceful means, but there is no indication at all, as far as I can see, that we are any nearer that situation. A nation without arms cannot fight. Some great shock was needed to compel the government to heed the voice of conscience. *This* is the shock."

He looked round at every man who heard him.

The girl said into Stefan's ear: "You're through, sir."

"Stefan?" Palfrey said.

Stefan whispered: "Domminy is delivering an ultimatum. Send men to the Cabinet room. We must hold him.

Palfrey said: "I didn't quite get that. Hold who?"

"*Domminy.*"

Domminy was looking at Stefan, and for the first time he unclasped his hands. His voice grew sharper.

"If you are attempting to send word to Palfrey or your other associates, you are wasting your time. I have made the necessary arrangements to have them rendered harmless at the Forest Hotel, in London, and wherever else they are working on this matter. I knew that you were endeavouring to find that very great scientist, Professor Rondivallo, and consequently I have been able to neutralize much of what you have attempted to do. I confess that I had not intended to act as quickly as I have. In another five or six weeks I think it would have been possible to control the paralytic outbreaks more thoroughly, and also control the severity, but the important thing is the shock which has been delivered. No man can be such a fool as to reject an ultimatum of this kind, which is delivered with the sole object of serving the best interests of mankind. Ah'm, Mr Prime Minister, I am going to suggest that you should contact all other Governments forthwith, either direct—which would gain time—or through the United Nations, which might in the long run be more effective, and inform them of the conditions which I have laid down. You must not attempt to molest me in any way. I have been nominated as the only negotiator for Professor

Rondivallo and his co-scientists, who would be very angry indeed if anything should happen to me."

He stopped, while still looking at the Prime Minister.

"There is little time, but possibly you would like to discuss this," he went on. "I shall be willing to give you any information you require so that you may judge the seriousness of what I have told you. For instance, you will wish to know how effectively a widespread re-occurrence of the plague could be handled. I assure you, most effectively.

"We have the facilities, the organization and the requirements in every town of any importance *throughout the world*.

"*Well*, Mr Prime Minister?"

BOOK III

THE PLAGUE

19. The Attack

PALFREY heard every word.

Some of it was faint, but every syllable came through, and so did the hushed horror in that room at Number 10. He heard Domminy's calm statement that arrangements had been made to neutralize Z5, and could believe that it was true. He sat with the others in the room overlooking the forest, listening tensely for the odd word which reached them. In the hotel everything seemed quiet.

Domminy finished.

Stefan said in a whisper: "Did you get it all, Sap?"

"Every word."

"Watch yourself."

"I will," Palfrey put the receiver down slowly and his hand strayed to the hair at his forehead. He began to twist a few strands round his forefinger. One man burst out:

"What is it, Sap. What's on?"

Palfrey said slowly: "Domminy is one of the leaders, George. No wonder we were forestalled nearly everywhere. At least we got moving today before he could stop us. He wants complete destruction of all armaments. The saint gone mad. He says he's arranging to neutralize us. That will almost certainly mean by the hotel residents and staff. They've let us have our head so far. Made quite a job of fooling us, too."

"We'd better scatter," George said abruptly. "Let's get a move on."

"Will it help?" Palfrey asked.

George said: "We can get Domminy——"

"If it's possible, Stefan will," Palfrey said. "But I can't

see Domminy doing this without being pretty sure of himself. Keep quiet a minute." He sat quite still except for the twisting fingers at his forehead, staring at the forest. The fire had died down and there was only a red glow to show where it had been, an occasional lick of flame. The headlamps were still on, spreading white light over the steps, the lawns, the flower beds. "He says that he and Rondivallo have agents in all large cities where they can start the plague if they want to," Palfrey went on. "Don't need telling what that means. Someone is in or near Lauriston, and he has counterpart in all large cities. What is common to all large cities, George?"

George said: "Sap, you're just talking for the sake of talking. Cut it out. Let's get away while we can."

Palfrey seemed to look through him.

"Water," he said. "The public services of all kinds. This infection could conceivably be from insects bred in polluted water, but there's no proof. What else? Shops. Laboratories. Factories. Workshops."

The door opened, and Sarak stepped in. He spoke at last, clearly, and quickly, in very broken English.

"The servants are disarming our men. Please."

"Let's get out of here!" George cried.

"Yes," said Palfrey, and stood up. "That's if they'll let us. What is common to all cities and common to Lauriston? Lauriston is just a little town."

"Come on, Sap!"

Palfrey said: "Take it easy, George," and brushed at something which touched his nose; as he did so, George flicked something away from the back of his hand, and Sarak waved his hand in front of his face.

"Please——" he began.

"My God!" breathed George, "the mosquitoes!" He slapped at two which lit upon his forehead, and then exclaimed: "Breath through your handkerchief!"

"You will all be bitten, and a bite will do the same

thing as a breath of the dust," said the fat, bulky-faced resident, coming heavily along the passage. "Including you, Palfrey. While you have time for reflection perhaps you will remember that it does not always pay to be offensive to people whom you think are quite helpless. None of your men is likely to escape. All of the staff and the residents are immune, of course, they have been subjected to a course of immunization. No doubt you would like to know that the immunization has been through food which everyone has eaten, and not everyone realized that they were being so treated."

George said: "Well, there's one of you who won't live to laugh about it."

He had an automatic in his hand.

"Put that away!" the bulky man said sharply. "If treated by our neutralizing agent you will recover in a week, but if you attempt violence you will not be treated. Then within a few hours you will be dead." He waved his hand, as if the threat of the gun was non-existent, and looked straight at Palfrey. "You will at least have the good sense to know that violence won't help you."

"Oh yes," said Palfrey. "Couldn't agree more."

George growled: "Well, I haven't."

He levelled the gun at the man, who seemed to realize that the danger was real. He reared up. Palfrey struck at George's right hand, but George was too far away. He fired twice. One bullet struck the bulky man in the forehead, another in the chest.

One moment he was alive, the next, he was dead on his feet.

"I'll show you how to get out of here," George said savagely. "I'll shoot as many of the swine as I see." He leapt towards the door and swung towards the main landing. He fired again and a man cried out. He went running, while Sarak stood quite still, looking up at Palfrey as if pleading with him to tell him what to do.

181

A mosquito landed on Palfrey's cheek and he felt a sharp pain. He squashed the insect, and as he did so, felt a burning sensation at the back of his throat. Sarak and the other two men began to cough.

A man called out from the passage: "No one else will get away with that. If you're carrying guns, throw them on the floor."

Palfrey said: "Yes," in a clipped voice, and took a gun out and dropped it. "Listen carefully," he said to the others as they drew near, and added in a whisper: "We've got to fool them, we haven't a chance to fight. I'm heading for the First Aid Room, where Matt is. Follow me one at a time. I'll wait there for five minutes." He stopped as a youthful-looking man appeared, one of those who had been on the verandah earlier in the evening. He looked vicious.

He said: "I'd like to cut your throat for killing him, but there's a better way to let you die." He stared at the red mark of the plague, and there was ferocity in his expression as he went on: "In half an hour you'll all be as helpless as new-born kittens. You'll be in agony."

He went down on one knee beside the bulky man, but he didn't speak again, didn't even take the flabby hand.

The dead man was the Smith who had ordered the murders of Korven and Dr Dimmock.

The young man said: "Pick him up. Carry him to his own room." He jumped to his feet and shouted: "Do what you're told, do something while you can move your bodies, you won't be able to much longer. *Pick him up!*"

"Where is his room?" Palfrey asked.

182

"Two along to the right. *Pick him up!*"

Palfrey said: "All right. Sarak, take his shoulders. Jim, come and help me. One of you help Sarak." Talking was an effort, and the burning pain was worse. He felt a twinge in his right leg, too. The others must be feeling much the same.

He moved towards the dead man's feet, and to do so he had to pass close to the younger man who seemed to take it for granted that there was no danger now.

Palfrey dropped his hand on to the other's wrist, and twisted. As the gun dropped, Sarak leapt forward. His hands went round the thin throat, choking all sound. No one else was in the passage.

The other Z5 men went to the doorway, and one went back for the guns. The man sagged, unconscious, his body a dead weight against Sarak, who let him fall.

"All right, we'll go altogether now," Palfrey said. He could only just get the words out. "Keep your guns out of sight, and don't talk if anyone tries to stop us." He led the way along the passage, and as he reached the hall he saw two girls, pretty young girls, laughing at a Z5 man who was standing between them on the stairs.

"It won't be long before you go dumb, Sammy," one of them said, "you won't ever be fresh with me again."

On the man's forehead were two dead mosquitoes.

Palfrey looked at the girls, and said: "You'll be all right Sam."

"All right!" a girl echoed, and laughed in his face. "That's all you know about it, Palfrey. Didn't you know you'd had a gnat bite?"

Palfrey didn't speak to her. His muscles were twitching and his throat burning.

A man at the foot of the stairs said sneeringly: "Not feeling sociable, Palfrey? Where do you think you're going?"

Palfrey said roughly: "If I'm going to die, I'll die outside. Get out of my way."

The man moved.

"Don't waste your time," he said, "you haven't got ten minutes left. Not even time to dig your own grave."

Palfrey turned towards the passage which led to some of the lounges, and to the first aid room. The others followed, and the man and the two girls were behind them, puzzled, keeping their distance. They believed that collapse would start at any moment, and they were right; there was only one thing they didn't know.

Palfrey opened the door of the first aid room and Matt Stone jumped up from the sofa.

Matt jumped up from the sofa.

20. The Escape

PALFREY managed to say painfully: "Matt, you can see what's happened to us. Don't talk." He moved to the shelf and pushed open a glass door, took down a hypodermic syringe and two small boxes. With great care, he filled a syringe, then injected Sarak, one other agent, and himself. "Must capture that helicopter," he added, "then get off in it. Our one hope. Feel all right?"

Matt said: "I've never felt fitter. That injection——"

"Saved you, can save us," Palfrey muttered. He put the automatic into Matt's hand. "Shoot your way to the helicopter. We'll be just behind you. Must get there while—while we can walk." He turned stiffly towards the door and opened it.

Matt went out and saw the man and the two girls, still watching. He went towards a door which led into the grounds. As he stepped outside two men came forward, and one said:

"Where do you think you're going?"

"Air," Palfrey gasped. "Must have air."

One of the men laughed.

"You'll get the air all right!" He stood aside, and as he moved, Matt struck him on the side of the head with the butt of the gun. He went down heavily. The other man opened his mouth to shout, but Sarak was on him like an avenging dog and choked his cry, then choked the breath out of him. Sarak was less affected than the others, but all could move.

"What's happening out there?" called the man from inside.

"Past white—building," Palfrey muttered to Matt, and turned to Sarak. "Stay back, Sarak. Take the—syringe. Inject—one other man if—if you get a chance. If they discover what we're doing——"

Sarak said heavily: "I will see to them all."

Matt Stone was moving freely, obviously quite cured —but he felt desperate even with the gun in his hand. Palfrey and the others looked ill and pain-wracked, likely to collapse at any moment. The one hope was that Rondivallo's men would assume that they would do so soon.

"Help—me," Palfrey gasped to Matt.

They pushed through a shrubbery to a clearing with the others close behind. Gaunt and silent in the star-light was the helicopter which had been used for the sortie into the forest. No one stood near it, no one was at the controls.

"Know how—to handle this one?" Palfrey asked.

"No. But I've handled helicopters."

Palfrey said: "Have to—learn fast."

Matt helped him into the cabin, then helped the others. He switched on a light. Other lights were shining from doorways, the beams of torches were waving about, some drawing nearer. Palfrey collapsed on to the pilot's seat. "Know the—general principle—of landing?"

"I can manage," Matt said.

He started the engine and the throbbing roar filled the cabin, the helicopter began to quiver. In front of Matt was a mass of controls.

"I'll give her a couple of minutes to warm up," Matt said. "Then we'll have to make it. They'll probably start firing at us soon."

That was when Palfrey felt the pain at his throat worse; then that he realized that he was going to lose his voice.

Palfrey said: "Right, we're airborne. You're on your own," he managed to add. "Remember the statue at Winchester. Not Lauriston, too dangerous. Winchester. Tell the police——"

His voice faded.

Matt said: "You take it easy, you'll be all right."

They were flying at about five hundred feet, and were over the forest. Below them, a great circle had been burned and was still glowing red, and the smoke still rose. They could smell the burning. Beyond were a few lights, almost certainly the lights of Conne village, and further away many more lights in a great cluster: Lauriston. To the east was Winchester, and he could imagine the lights there but wasn't sure that he could pick them out.

Matt felt the throbbing of the engine, louder and fiercer. Turning his head, he could see the Forest Hotel, ablaze with light, and yet it looked so far away that it seemed in a different world. Lauriston drew nearer. Conne fell away, on the right. The lights of Winchester itself became quite bright. Road speeds were so trivial against air speed, even the comparative slowness of the helicopter. Eighty miles an hour meant twenty miles in a quarter of an hour, and that was the time it should take to get to Winchester. They had been airborne for fully five minutes now; a third of the time. The forest seemed to be thinning out below them, they saw more cottages with lighted windows, and could make out the paleness of meadows and of fields of corn. Matt could discern great orchards, too.

Palfrey sat helpless and still in the seat next to Matt. The others were sitting against the fuselage, and neither of them could move or speak. There was only the throbbing roar for company: that, the hope that they would land safely and the fear that they would crash.

Matt kept thinking of people.

Yvonne.

Kathleen O'Shea.

The Larsens.

Hill, crashing in that little car.

The Carters. Why had they been killed? Had it been because Mrs Carter had seen Jane Hill examined by Dr Korven, and talked to her husband about it?

Why had this part of England been selected?

Why had the plague been released here? How was it carried? Where did the mosquitoes breed?

He thought of Yvonne again, her cold aloofness, the fact that she had hardly spoken to him, and had only once looked as if she might relax a little and smile. Then he pictured her as she had tried to get out of the car but had been nearly helpless, with that red smudge on her forehead.

Stop thinking about that. Winchester lay ahead, and Lauriston only a mile or so to the right. He could pick out the street lamps, the lighted windows and, to his surprise, the great sheds of the giant canning factory and freezing plant, the arclights which floodlit the plant, whenever it was on night shift. It was now. What had he been told by that gatekeeper? No night shift? He'd been wrong then, they were undoubtedly working a night shift, he could see the lights, the bright windows all over the place. It could never have been busier.

He glanced at Palfrey.

Palfrey was actually moving his lips. Palfrey was completely under the effect of the plague, his body was absolutely still, he could not turn his head, but he was moving his lips. Was he making any sound? The engine would drown it, anyhow, there was no way of making sure.

Palfrey actually leaned forward a fraction of an inch in his seat, to look out and down towards the packing station, and the great expanse of the Wide World Foods buildings. He seemed to be nodding his head.

The others were as still as death.

What was Palfrey trying to say?

Palfrey's mind was crystal clear. He had realized the truth the moment he had seen the glow of light over the Wide World plants: truth which he had suspected when he had realized that many of the Wide World staff lived at the Forest Hotel. Domminy's treachery had virtually proved the case, for Domminy had been with Wide World since it began its experimental work, had fought for Government subsidies to finance it.

There were Wide World Canning plants, freezing plants and packing plants all over the world; and depots for their canned and deep frozen foods were everywhere.

Everywhere.

The company's fine fruits, fine vegetables and agricultural produce of remarkable quality were in every town. It was almost possible to hear Domminy talking about the finest foods grown with the best fertilizers to produce the best results, on the radio, on television, in the House.

And he, Palfrey, could not talk or move to write, and did not know how long it would be before he could.

If he recovered as quickly as Matt Stone, then he might be in time.

Whatever Domminy was planning for the next stage would be started by now; it might be too late to stop him.

The Cabinet could not yield to that ultimatum; no Government could. There might be consultations with other Governments, talk, half promises; and some small countries might want to yield. But in a world without arms any group of people with arms could dominate the rest.

The military must raid Wide World.

And here they were, approaching Winchester, still at about five hundred feet. The lights of the city showed vividly. He could see those clearly enough, but could not see Matt Stone's face, because Matt was out of his range of vision. He could see Matt's hands and the complicated control panel.

There was the main street, wide at one end near the statue of King Alfred which looked like a toy soldier. Matt was slowing down. He was turning the helicopter. He was heading for the statue, and seemed quite confident.

Matt said: "Going down."

He moved the control stick and felt the helicopter shuddering as it dropped straight down out of the skies. He could see people scuttling away from the pavements. One moment the statue was in sight, the next it vanished. Big buildings were on one side and several cars parked near it. He thought that he could see the shimmering waters of a river, but could not be sure.

If they overshot, if they crashed into one of the buildings, into a shop——

Palfrey felt the helicopter jolt upwards, and knew that he was flung upwards a little, but he wasn't flung out of his seat. Nor was Matt Stone. The whole machine was quivering, but it wasn't moving, it hadn't crashed.

If only he could speak.

Hadn't the injection worked?

21. The Plant

EVERY light that could be switched on was on in the Lauriston plant of the Wide World Foods Corporation. The night shift had been summoned that afternoon for special work in all departments, but there was particular concentration in the despatching of canned and frozen goods. Practically nothing else was going out. More and more huge insulated cans were being loaded at the loading platforms. Special trains had been ordered, and wagons were being filled by gangs of men working steadily and eagerly. In the landing fields the Corporation's aircraft were being made ready to carry the frozen and canned foods to all parts of the north and Scotland, to Ireland, and to parts of Western Europe.

The men looked unreal with the pallid green lights on them. They worked with a steady rhythm which was helped by the music from loud speakers placed at vantage points all over the plant, inside and outside; they were far enough from Lauriston to cause no nuisance. Here and there, men were humming.

The office buildings were in the middle of the plant, a modern block, housing a daytime staff of nearly a hundred; now, only a skeleton office staff was on duty, but the managing director's office was occupied.

Everyone who passed it could see the lights at the windows.

Inside were three men and a woman.

The office light fell on the woman's light auburn hair and the freshness of her complexion; she was no more than twenty-three or four, and if anyone of Palfrey's men saw her he would know that her name was O'Shea. She sat at the side of the biggest of the three men, a massive, barrel-shaped man with a conical head and small, pursed lips; the kind of man who might be dismissed as an intellectual lightweight because his forehead seemed so small.

The men each had a telephone in front of them, and two were speaking into the telephone, one in Arabic, the other in Hungarian. Each spoke swiftly, and each made notes against a typewritten sheet in front of him. The girl, Maureen O'Shea, was writing numbers by the side of entries on other typewritten sheets. She looked as cool as she was lovely. Now and again she glanced at the fat man, whether he was looking at her or not.

Once she said: "How much longer will it take?"

"My dear, don't ask me," Rondivallo said absently. "We should have had much more time, but who could know it? Eh? Who could know?" He was studying a map of the world, which was pinned to a board in front of him. Every now and again he glanced at one of the papers on either side, from which the men were working, and made a little red dot on the map. From time to time he smoothed down his forehead and ran his hand over the bald scalp, making a little hissing noise; he had only a fringe of black hair at the temples and the back of his head. He wore pince nez, and kept wrinkling his nose.

The two men finished one conversation and immediately started another, each into a telephone, each in a different language, now Spanish and Swedish; their grasp of each language was quite remarkable. The Spanish-speaking man finished first and put the telephone down, but immediately picked it up again, and said:

"Yes . . . Canada, yes." Now he began to talk in English, with a very slight accent. "Yes, the supplies are on their way to you," he said. "You need only the spawn of course, you will find that the mushrooms are quite remarkable." He did not smile, his expression was one of extreme earnestness, as he went on: "Operations are likely to begin tomorrow evening and should start in Ottawa, Winnipeg and Vancouver . . . No, not elsewhere until you have further instructions. Thank you."

He rang off; picked up the telephone again, and began to speak in Chinese; now he spoke more slowly, as if at last there was a language with which he was not thoroughly familiar.

This time he put the receiver down more slowly, looked up, then ran his hand across his forehead and left a streak of finger marks across the film of sweat. The other man was still speaking. Rondivallo had pushed his chair back. He yawned, and tapped his mouth with the tips of his long, pale fingers. Maureen O'Shea jumped up quickly.

"Are we going to have supper"

"Supper?" echoed Rondivallo, and drummed his fingers on his forehead as he looked at her; his mouth puckered into a smile. "Yes, yes, I will have a little food, but you worry about me too much, Maureen, I have had to stand much greater pressures than these. Why, we are on the point of success, the very point of success!" Behind the pince nez his eyes glistened. "When we began I was afraid that we had timed it badly, that we needed more time, but——" he shrugged his sloping shoulders. "All will be well."

He tapped his pockets, and the girl took cigarettes out of her bag and lit one, and handed it to him.

The other two men watched.

"Thank you, thank you," Rondivallo said. "Yes, all

192

will be well, my dear, we shall not have laboured in vain. And you will be able to live in the world again, you won't have to be cooped up any longer; but it's been worth it, now, hasn't it? If they'd found you they would have found me, and—well, forget it, forget it. It's nearly over."

His eyes glistened so much.

"Are you sure they will all give in?" Maureen asked, almost hesitantly.

Rondivallo's voice grew sharp.

"Of course they will. What choice have they? Either begin at once to destroy their arms, or be visited by a plague which can wipe them out. Even if the Governments don't wish to do it, my dear, the people will compel them to, and we shall have nothing more to worry about." He paused to draw at the cigarette, then to move about the modern office, with its angled furniture and its concealed lighting, which gave almost the brightness of day. Yet there was nothing at all nervous in his pacing. "The Government of this country will impose a censorship immediately of course, and nothing will be said over the British Broadcasting Corporation's stations, but we shall broadcast from our small stations effectively enough to make sure that all the people know that the disaster *can* be stopped. The Government's earlier measures, aimed at steadying the country, induced panic more than anything else. So everyone will be most receptive." His lips puckered again. "I expect to hear from Domminy soon."

"Won't they arrest him?" Maureen asked.

The other two men glanced at each other, as if that fear had been on their minds, too.

"Of course they won't," said Rondivallo testily. "Why don't you use your mind, Maureen? They will allow him to stay free, hoping that he will lead them to us, but what a hope they have!" He chuckled and his whole face lit up. "He will talk to us by radio and they will have some job tracing us that way! Everything else is in excellent order. Palfrey and his Z5 men are helpless at the Forest Hotel and in London. Every country in the world has received the ultimatum, and they will give way. They will *have* to give way."

Abruptly, his mood changed, and he scowled.

"If they delay, then there will have to be a very sharp lesson. If they delay, then I shall give our London agent the word to act. Already there are big supplies of infected foods at Covent Garden, all tomorrow morning's deliveries will be infected, and as the fruit and vegetables are taken into the homes, the bacteria will develop. Some will grow even before that. All tomorrow's deliveries of frozen foods throughout London will also be infected. What a miracle," he breathed, "what a miracle! The moment these insects begin to feel the warmth of light rays whether in water or not, they will grow: and in a matter of minutes they will begin to fly."

Maureen said slowly: "Must you begin with London?"

"Of course I must!" The fat scientist's voice was sharp again. "Where else could the example be so effective? Once the world's other capital cities hear of what has happened—but I hope that it will not be necessary, my dear. I hope that Domminy will be able to persuade his fellow Cabinet Ministers that delay will be quite useless."

As abruptly as he had started to scowl, Rondivallo began to laugh. The laughter shook his big body and his flabby chins. He put a hand on Maureen's shoulder and clutched her tightly, as if in need of support. The two men smiled at him, but Maureen stared as if she could not understand.

"Oh, dear me, how funny it is," he said at last, and used a little finger to wipe the tears of laughter out of his eyes. "How very funny, my dear. Such a good man as Domminy helping us! Oh, he is a little mad, like all fanatics, but this upright, moral, righteous man believes

194

that it is the only way to take freedom to the world. Oh, my dear, what fools men can be, what fools they can be."

"Isn't it the way to freedom from fear?" Maureen asked, and her eyes were very steady.

"For you, yes." Rondivallo hugged her. "For me, yes. For everyone who is with us, yes. But to others, no. My dear Maureen, you must be a realist. Men will always fight, so they must be kept constantly under the threat of fear. Men must be governed and if necessary must be rigidly and ruthlessly compelled to submit to higher intelligences. Could you hope to make them do so in their present state of development? Can you imagine different peoples really living together in complete harmony? With their conflicting religions, their hatreds and prejudices, with all the centuries of enmity behind them, and with the rawness of the memory of recent events in their minds? Left to their own they will start quarreling and then fighting among themselves, and where will that get us? Where will it get you and *me*? Do you think I have worked these years so that I could allow the ordinary people, the politicians, the religious fanatics, the moralists, to start their silly quarrels again?"

He broke off, for a light flashed at a cabinet in one corner of the room. He looked and moved towards it with an arm round the girl's shoulder.

"Larsen thought that I had done that," he went on. "He was told only today what I really plan, and said that he would tell Domminy. Luckily Smith was able to make sure he didn't live to tell anyone. He should have known better, anyhow, and so should you, my dear. We have the military, naval and air strength to impose our will on the rest of the world for generations."

The light flickered.

"*We* have?" Maureen breathed.

"Yes," said Rondivallo, standing close to the cabinet and watching the flickering light. "In this very plant we have all the weapons needed to dominate the whole of this country. In each of our other plants we have what is needed to maintain effective control in other countries. First, the nations must lay down their arms. After that they will do what we tell them."

"What *you* tell them?" Maureen said.

He glanced down at her, and gave her another little squeeze. "Yes, that is right. Good girl! What *I* tell them." He chuckled. "Everyone who serves me has to obey, because they know that with other infections, such as the present plague, I can dispose of them. *Phutt!* Those who kill me kill everything. And I have given the order for the attack on London to begin unless I cancel it, so—I had better not die. Eh, Maureen? Now, here is a message. It will be from Domminy."

The other two men had moved and were standing in front of the cabinet, which looked like a small radiogram, with a small loudspeaker built in.

A man's voice came, clearly.

"This is Juno speaking, Juno speaking, please stand by for a report."

"Juno?" Rondivallo frowned. "What does the Forest Hotel want now? Don't they realize that we are too busy to be worried by small matters?"

No one else spoke.

The same voice came through the loud speaker again.

"This is Juno speaking, Juno speaking. This is to inform you that Dr Palfrey and three of his men escaped twenty minutes ago, using a Civil Defence helicopter. One of the men was not affected by the mosquito bite, and may be capable of aggressive action. Palfrey and the other two men were bitten, but Palfrey is now known to have taken a hypodermic syringe and a distillation of curare with him. He may know that if injected subcutaneously the curare will protect him against the full paralytic effects. Message ends. This is Juno speaking, Juno standing by to receive your instructions.

Rondivallo had lost every vestige of colour. The perspiration was standing out on his forehead and glistened on his neck. He snatched at a microphone attached to the cabinet, and said hoarsely:

"Which direction did they go"

"In the general direction of Lauriston and Winchester."

"How long ago?"

"Twenty minutes."

Rondivallo slapped the microphone back into position and swung round.

"We must locate that helicopter and destroy it and everyone in it," he said. "Mikki, arrange for two of our aircraft to search for it and to attack with guided missiles at once *At once, do you hear me?*"

One of the two men turned and ran towards the door.

Matt Stone saw the dozens of people gathered on the ground near the King Alfred statue, some crouching, some standing up, one or two shaking a fist. Two policemen came stalking towards the helicopter itself, neither dawdling nor hurrying. Matt stood up and stepped towards the sliding door. A peg kept it in position. He took the peg out and pushed the door back as the policemen appeared, craning their necks, the tops of their helmets level with the bottom of the door.

"You've got all of Hampshire to land in, what made you choose this place?" one demanded.

Matt said:

"I must see the chief of police right away. It's so desperate that minutes might make a difference between living and dying."

"That sounds very serious, sir." The policeman was ponderous. "Will you please explain more."

He broke off, staring past Matt towards Palfrey. Matt saw his astonishment and looked round quickly.

Palfrey was stretching out his arms to clutch the instrument panel, so as to pull himself up. His lips were working, as a man's who has some grave impediment, and when he spoke his voice seemed strange and uncanny; yet the words were clear.

"Call—on—help—for—Z5. Arrange—military—block—all—roads—out of—Lauriston. Take—me—nearest—military—authority."

He thrust his card forward.

"Understand?"

"Z5."

The policeman looked at the card, and said in a strained voice: "Very good, Dr Palfrey, I understand."

Five minutes later Palfrey was moving and talking with comparative freedom, and the other man was beginning to regain his power of movement and of speech. Police cars came up. Matt got in, Palfrey was helped in, and they moved off, while a crowd of dozens of people grew into a crowd of hundreds, gathering round the helicopter, peering into it, seeing the slight damage where it had scraped against the base of the statue of King Alfred. They heard an aeroplane high above, and heard a little, hollow sound, like a succession of beats on a slack drum. Several, looking up, saw flashes in the sky.

They saw nothing else.

There was a sharp explosion and a blinding flash, as guided rockets struck the helicopter. It smashed into a flaming wreckage, and it was as if a great fire had swept over the people there, so that none was left alive.

But Palfrey lived.

22. Night of Dread

THE Commanding officer at the army base a few miles outside Winchester sat at his desk in a small office, with Palfrey and Matt Stone, and half a dozen aides. Sentries were posted at the door and the windows, messengers were constantly moving in and out. A fully-manned radio transmitter was in the next room, and messages were being sent out fast upon each other. The C.O. was a man in the early fifties, tall, laconic, slow speaking.

There was a lull for the first time since Palfrey and Matt Stone had arrived.

Army patrols were already on the road to Lauriston, and all roads out of Lauriston were being blocked. Jet and propeller flights were already taking off, to patrol the skies above the Wide World Foods Plant. Messages had gone out to have all depots and warehouses of Wide World Foods sealed off. Plans were already in hand to warn all shopkeepers and all market men who dealt with Wide World to isolate all such stocks of fresh, canned, processed and frozen foods. It had been like a military operation carried out with great precision and a minimum of fuss. Not once had the C.O. raised his voice, and now that there was a lull, and they were waiting for word from London, he looked upat a subaltern and said calmly:

"Lay on drinks and coffee, and you'd better arrange for some sandwiches for Dr Palfrey and his friends."

"Yes, sir." The subaltern saluted, clicked his heels, turned, went out at the double.

The C.O. smiled faintly.

"How long are you going to wait for word from London before deciding what to do next?" he asked. "We've the forces here to take over that food plant in half an hour, of course—less, if it comes to that. No problem."

Palfrey was almost his normal self again. He was smoking, and was playing with a few strands of hair; Matt could picture him sitting behind his own desk, instead of the upright chair; could imagine him talking to Stefan Andromovitch in that calm, thoughtful voice. But Matt knew Palfrey better now.

"Wish I could agree that it's no problem," Palfrey said. "If there were no other worry, there are the mosquitoes. They'd be made to swarm among any attacking group." He glanced at the door, and Matt not only understood but shared his dread.

The Commanding officer was so completely sure of himself.

"We'll send in squads trained and equipped for anti-gas and bacteria warfare," he declared. "No problem at all. We've two battalions fully equipped to fight in radio-active territory. Soon deal with those mosquitoes and the infernal dust!" He smiled more broadly. "My view is that I should send the men in at once."

"Get 'em ready, anyhow," Palfrey said. "I'm hoping that Andromovitch will have heard more, and can tell what's being done at Cabinet level."

A subaltern came in, approached the desk and saluted; and stared at the C.O. in a way which drove the smile away from the man's lips.

"Yes, Bob?"

"I've just received a report from Winchester, sir," the subaltern said. "Three of a party of twelve men on late pass have returned. They state that the other nine were killed when a helicopter was fired on from the air and destroyed in Winchester, sir."

Palfrey breathed: "No means of defence!"

The C.O. said very slowly: "Very well." He looked round at his officers and sat upright. "We shall prepare immediately for an offensive action on the Lauriston plant without waiting for approval from London or Command Headquarters. How long do you need to be ready?"

"Twenty minutes, sir."

"Anti-gas and bacterial warfare units must be ready."

"They are, sir, all but the finishing touches."

"Fine," said the C.O. and glanced at Palfrey. "We haven't any alternative."

He broke off.

The aide who had taken the instructions reached the doorway, where the two armed guards stood to attention. As he stepped into the night, he waved his hand in front of his face: and at the same moment one of the guards moved, backing away and wafting at something which had flown into his face. Then the doorway seemed filled with tiny flying insects, their wings catching the light, and their buzzing taking on a strange note of power. With them was a great cloud of dust.

The C.O. said: "My God!" He jumped to his feet, waving his hand in front of his face, while the other officers dodged back and sideways, beating widly at the air.

"Where else is it happening?" Palfrey asked in a savage voice. "Where else?" He stood up and went into the radio room, with the C.O. close behind him, and the officers in the other room looking at each other in horror, each with the mark of the plague upon him. "Have all possible camps and bases warned, all Commands notified, the War Ministry and Naval and Air Force authorities warned," he said. "Will you give the orders, sir?"

"Yes. Jones, get me Command Headquarters, General Rampling himself. Palfrey, how long have I got before I feel the effects?"

"Ten or fifteen minutes at most," Palfrey said.

"Should be enough. Colonel Wray!" The C.O. raised his

voice, and one of the officers came hurrying. "See if we can rustle up a squad or so of men not yet infected; and who have got into protective clothing."

"Yes, sir."

"You've nine minutes," the C.O. said dryly. "All right, Sergeant Jones, the moment——" he broke off, as Jones looked round, a fresh-faced youth with red cheeks and frightened eyes. He had just squashed a mosquito on the switchboard, but did not yet seem to have been affected himself. "What is it?" the C.O. demanded.

"A Mr Drommich, for Dr Palfrey, sir."

"Andromovitch!" Palfrey exclaimed. "Let me talk to him." He snatched up a pair of earphones which Sergeant Jones indicated, while Jones said to the C.O. "General Rampling is on the air, sir."

"Thanks," the C.O. boomed. Then: "Percy, Micky here! I don't want to be an alarmist, but . . ."

As he spoke, the swelling on his forehead and the back of his hands grew larger, and his voice began to fade.

And Palfrey talked, too.

Matt studied Palfrey's face as he did so, seeing the tension and great dread.

Palfrey had the earphones on, and was standing with his shoulders stooping a little. He seemed to listen for a long time, and his expression did not ease. Matt felt his own tension rising to screaming point; he could hear the C.O.'s voice from time to time, giving a flat factual report, but what he wanted to hear was the Russian.

Palfrey said at last:

"All right, Stefan, there might be half a chance. I'll take it if I can." He rang off, took the earphones away quickly, and moved across and gripped the C.O.'s arm. The C.O. shook him off, then saw who it was, and said more sharply into the radio telephone:

"Just a minute, Percy. Hallo, Palfrey?"

"I'd like any men you've got who're not affected and

202

have protective clothing, with small arms, including sub-machine guns, hand grenades, tear gas and fire bombs. Quickly."

"Right. Soames!" The Colonel raised his voice only a little; it squeaked. "Soames, get Dr Palfrey what he's just asked for." A major was standing in the doorway, rubbing at the swelling on his forehead. "Just pass on instructions that Palfrey may have——"

He paused.

He gulped.

For the first time something like fear showed in his eyes, but he gulped again, and then made himself go on in a constricted voice:

". . . anything he requires. Hurry." He turned back to the radio phone. "Percy, my throat's beginning to close up. I won't—be able—to—talk—much."

He stopped.

Then he said in tones of horror: "Oh, my God!" and looked at Palfrey, who was already at the door. "Command has been attacked by swarms of the mosquitoes."

He winced, tried to speak again, but could not utter a sound.

A soldier with a hood which draped down from his steel helmet, and wearing protective clothing, came hurrying towards the Commanding officer's office. His voice sounded muffled, but Palfrey and Matt could make out the words quite clearly.

"Dr Palfrey, sir?"

"Yes."

"I'm Lance-Corporal Pollitt, sir. I have two armour-protected trucks, three jeeps and a staff car available, with twenty men, all in fighting order. Two Bren guns, four sub-machine guns, good supplies of grenades, two flame throwers and ample small arms, sir." There was a moment's pause, before he burst out: "All raring to go."

"Right," Palfrey said. "We won't take the staff car. We're liable to air attack and that wouldn't give us a chance. Ready to leave now?"

"Yes, sir."

"Head for Lauriston, but avoid main roads where you can," Palfrey said. "Know the district?"

"Been manoeuvring round here for three years, sir, know it like the palm of my hand."

"Good. I'll go in the first armoured truck, with Mr Stone here." Palfrey turned to the two Z5 men who had landed with the helicopter, and said quietly: "You two can find more than enough to do. If you can get any supplies of curare distillate it would help if it's injected subcutaneously within half an hour." He could say that quite calmly, hiding the horror or the truth: that there could only be supplies for a few of the men, and the plague might kill nine out out of ten.

"Okay, Sap," one of them said. "Luck."

The engines of the armoured trucks and jeeps were roaring, the men climbing in. Lance-Corporal Pollit gave Palfrey a hand inside one of the armoured trucks, then helped Matt up. There was just room to sit. Four other men crouched at the back, and the car was loaded with ammunition. Matt thought of what could happen if a single shell pierced the armour plating.

A dim light showed inside the car as they began to move off.

The lance-corporal said:

"We've protection clothing for you gents too, sir."

"Thanks. We'll take a helmet each," Palfrey said. "We're freaks, we're immune. Do you know where the mosquitoes came from?"

"Perishing kitchens, sir, cookhouse if you know what I mean." He grinned beneath his gauze protective drapes. "First I heard of it, couple of orderlies on fatigue duty come and said there was a swarm of mosquitoes coming out of the spuds they were peeling.

New delivery, only came in this afternoon. Before we knew where we were, they were all over the place. I've always been sensitive to skeeters, sir, and they make me itch like hell, and besides that I'd heard the news. So I nipped back quick to put on protective clothing, and told these boys to do the same, sir. Better safe than sorry, if you know what I mean."

"I know," said Palfrey. "A lot of people might live to be grateful to that bit of quick thinking."

"Truth is, I had the wind up, sir. Still have, if it comes to that." Pollit looked at the back of the driver as they passed out of the camp, and saw two sentries reeling back from their posts as if they had been attacked by the insect swarms. "Think we've any chance of stopping it spreading, sir? Seems a hell of a thing. Everything okey-doke one minute, and this the next."

"There's a chance," Palfrey said. "We're making it."

They might be stopped before they reached the Wide World Foods plant.

Even if they reached the plant, he could not be sure of what he could do, he could only follow his instinct to get to the heart of the trouble.

He did not know what was happening up and down the country.

No one did.

Spasmodic reports were received in London, by Andromovitch and by the Cabinet, but there was a state of hopeless confusion over most of the country. The facts which did emerge were so frightening that it was almost unbearable to contemplate them. Dozens of military establishments of all kinds had been invaded by swarms of the mosquitoes and satellites all coming from the food stores or the cookhouses. Except for small isolated units, the armed forces were at a standstill in many parts of the country. No effective counter measures had yet been taken. The one piece of information which offered some hope was that the bacteriological life seemed short; scientists in a dozen research laboratories had established that they had a total life span of twelve hours. No other news was even slightly encouraging. Some army units which had left their stations before the plague had struck had held up Wide World Food lorries and vans, but in every case they had been attacked by the plague within minutes.

So far, all of this had taken place in country districts or in garrison towns and dockyards and naval bases. None of the other large cities had yet been affected to any serious degree. But the exodus towards the coast, by sea and by air, had become a stupendous shift of population, as radio messages from unidentified stations conveyed news of the ultimatum, and kept news of the catastrophe to the armed services circulating all the time. Rumour fed upon rumour.

And in London, little Domminy, with his fuzzy ring of hair and his skinny hands, was telling the Cabinet that it had no choice. The armed forces were helpless; the armed forces of other nations would be, soon, unless the weapons were destroyed. No weapon was any use without its men to man it, he pointed out in his flat, almost querulous voice. The order to accept the ultimatum should be given immediately, and other countries should be advised to take the same step.

What did the Cabinet want?

To massacre the whole population?

"And let it be understood," he said waspishly, "that if I am arrested or detained, you will have no one left to convey your decisions to my colleagues, and my colleagues are in many parts of the country and many parts of the world. This is a time for unconditional surrender, Mr Prime Minister. I hope that you will realize that in time to stop the slaughter!"

Stop the slaughter, cried the people.
Stop the slaughter, cried the newspapers.
Stop the slaughter, boomed the radio.
Stop the slaughter, pleaded television.
Stop the slaughter, slaughter, slaughter.

Then a new voice came, whispering at first:

"No one need suffer once the Government has taken the sensible course, and submitted to certain conditions which will lead to a complete free democratic world. No one need suffer, because there is a way to arrest the paralysis and return to complete health, a simple preparation available in vast quantities. No one need suffer, once the Government accepts the terms."

Stop the slaughter.
Stop the slaughter.

"Hear that, sir?" Lance-Corporal Pollitt asked.

"Hear what?"

"There's a local station broadcasting that if the Government gives way, everyone who has been infected can be cured. Bloody lie, I bet."

"Any idea where it's coming from?"

"No, sir. Sparks says that it's a weak local station, calls itself World Wide."

"Sounds right," said Palfrey. "How far are we from Lauriston?"

"Three miles, sir."

"Main road?"

"Yes, sir, but there's another road, takes us further round, leads to the railway station, and Wide World Plant is built with railway sidings. There's a private road from the station into the plant. If it comes to that, we could go along the railway track itself, they wouldn't be expecting us that way."

"Do that," Palfrey said.

Pollit gave the driver instructions; the other cars would

follow this one. Palfrey leaned back against the side, with his head bumping against the roof of the armoured truck all the time, eyes half closed, a cigarette dangling from his lips. He seemed free from tension. He wasn't dozing, just relaxing while he could.

He took an automatic pistol from a case by his side and handed it to Matt.

"Special army issue," he said, and pointed to a box. "Spare ammo there."

"Thanks." Matt felt a kind of security as he put the gun into his pocket, and saw Palfrey pocket one.

After a while Matt said very slowly and quietly:

"Sap."

Palfrey didn't even turn his head.

"Yes?"

"Think there's any hope that it's true?"

"The cure?"

"Yes."

"Whoever is behind this can't want to massacre a nation," said Palfrey. "Whatever they plan, they'll want men and women to work. Yes, I think there's a cure, but whether there's enough to stop disaster if the plague spreads too far——"

He didn't finish.

Lance-Corporal Pollitt said quietly: "We're turning into the road near the station, sir, and the lights of the Wide World plants are just ahead. See the lights, sir?"

Palfrey said: "Yes, I can see."

As he finished, the driver jammed on his brakes, while men shouted at them from the railway and the road, and a shot rang out, sharp and clear.

23. Rondivallo

Pollitt was on his feet almost before the sound of the shot had died away, and two men were already jumping down from the back of the armoured truck. Palfrey heard two more shots and then a sharp explosion; the truck seemed to sway. Pollitt dropped over the back as the car came to a standstill. The driver said:

"All right to stop, sir?"

"Get on," Palfrey said. "We want to get into the heart of the plant."

"Right, sir."

Pollitt shouldn't have gone.

He was clambering back.

"Ran into a patrol of three men, sir, that's three of the devils less. How many d'you think there are?"

"We'd better assume there's a whole army, probably most of the workers here. They'd only call in men they thought they could trust for a shift tonight."

"Special instructions of any kind, sir?"

"We've got to get through," said Palfrey simply. He bent his head to peer through the windscreen. Ahead lay the brightly lit plant, and he believed that he could hear engines roaring, probably those of aircraft preparing to take off. Cars were moving in the distance. The light from the big sheds of the plant looked almost like daylight. He could see a high fence on one side, and just ahead was a platform, with great piles of packing cases on it. Nearby, men were loading wagons in the light of powerful floodlights which showed them as dark silhouettes. One or two of them turned to look at the truck. The driver bumped the wheels over the track, drove past the loading platform and the working men, and turned into the grounds of the plant. Most of the great buildings were ablaze with light. The plant was built round a great courtyard, and in the middle was a huge building with many of its windows in darkness, although it was floodlit. One word showed up clearly over the doorway:

OFFICES

Two or three men came hurrying from the entrances to the other buildings, and one carried a rifle. The truck came to a standstill.

"Leave this to me, sir," Pollitt said.

He jumped out, flinging back the net which draped over his face. The other three soldiers with Palfrey and Matt Stone were crouching at the ready, and keeping their leader covered. There was a sharp exchange of words, then Pollitt moved towards the man with a rifle like a terrier at a rat. Palfrey saw the victim stagger and then fall, saw Pollitt wrench the rifle away from him, swing round, and crack it on the head of one of the other two men. One of the soldiers jumped down, tommygun at the ready, covering the third man, who backed away.

But others came hurrying from entrances of the different plants, and there was the sharp crack of a shot.

"*Keep them back!*" roared Pollitt.

The men at the back of the truck began to fire, sweeping their guns round, bullets pecking the concrete courtyard just in front of the advancing men. Others came running, from doorways and from corners, and were met by the withering fire. Men began to fall. Others began to fire back, but spasmodically, as yet they had no automatic weapons.

"We'll make a run for it," Palfrey said, as quietly as if he was talking of dodging a shower of rain. "All set, Matt?"

"Ready."

"Make for the office entrance," said Palfrey, "and give Pollitt a chance to cover us." He swung down, and

210

Matt was close on his heels. They ran towards the office block entrance, while bullets began to hum. Matt felt a sharp pain at his right shoulder, but it didn't last long and wasn't enough to stop him. Palfrey reached the open doorway a yard ahead, and as he did so, two men lunged at him from inside.

Matt's heart seemed to jump into his throat and choke him. If these were armed——

They were not.

Palfrey shot one of them in the chest, Matt the other in the throat. They fell away. Palfrey swung round as the shooting slackened outside. There came a clatter of footsteps, and Pollitt and two of his men came running, with hand grenades swinging from their belts. The two men had tommy guns, Pollitt a rifle.

"One of you keep 'em out," he said to the men, "the other follow us. Which floor, sir, d'you know?"

"No."

"I'll find out." Pollitt swung round to one of the men on the floor. It was bright in here, and everything in the wounded man's expression and in Pollitt's was clearly visible; just then Pollitt was the most ruthless man in the world.

"We want Rondivallo and the redhead," Palfrey said thinly. "Where are they?"

The wounded man's lips twisted.

"We want Rondivallo and the redhead, and if you don't tell us where they are I'll make you think that bullet just kissed you. *Where are they?*"

"The—third floor," the man gasped. "Third floor."

It was strangely quiet up here.

The lift had stopped at a wide landing, with a door on either side. One was marked: *Directors.* Pollit, the one private, Matt and Palfrey went toward it, and Palfrey said:

"Leave your man here, will you?"

"Yes, sir. Dicky, keep everyone out, even if it means blowing yourself up. Understand?"

"Okay, Polly."

"I'll Polly you," Pollitt growled. "Want me to go ahead, sir? Better allow me." He pushed towards the door marked *Directors*. It was still strangely silent, as if everything had stopped in the courtyard, but here were thick windows, and he could actually see the flashes from men who were shooting at the lone soldiers down below. Then he saw another armoured truck come into the range of the floodlights; reinforcements which might make the difference between life and death.

To Palfrey?

To Matt?

To millions?

Pollitt kicked open the door, and it opened on to a wide passage. The windows were in the main wall on one side, a pale blue wall was on the other, broken with doorways. Over each door were words, such as: *Chairman, Secretary, Board Room, Operations Room.*

Pollitt opened the doors one by one, peering inside each, the rifle at the ready; but until they reached the operations room each was empty.

He opened this door slowly, and the sound of a voice came clearly.

"We warned them, we couldn't have warned them more clearly, don't blame me."

Blame?

Pollitt stood aside, without making a sound. Palfrey went to the door, with Matt close behind him. They saw four people standing between a large desk and what looked like a radio cabinet. One of the men, Rondivallo, was glaring at a girl who, even from the back, looked

212

remarkably like Kathleen O'Shea. For a wild moment Matt thought it was; then he saw her profile, and realized that this was Maureen.

The two men were staring at Rondivallo.

The girl was standing two yards away from him.

She said in a tense, frightened voice: "You told me no one would suffer, you told me it was just a way to frighten people. Now you've killed—you've killed thousands. You're worse than the Devil himself." She crossed herself as she drew further back, and while Rondivallo glared at her.

"Why, you little fool, what did you think would happen? I had to teach them a lesson, didn't I? I had to make them realize that I meant business. And what did they do? They sent the whole army after me! They started to hold up our trucks and vans and even raided our warehouses. I had to strike, I had to make them realize that they hadn't a chance. *Don't you interrupt me!*" He raised his right hand, clenched, as if he would come forward and strike her. "I warned them, I said I would destroy the whole of the armed forces, and that's what I've done. And if the rest of the nations don't get rid of their weapons quickly, they'll be wiped out, too. I can't stop *now*. Victory's within my grasp, don't you understand that? Why, you redheaded little bitch, you could be queen of the world!"

"I don't want to be queen of the world," Maureen O' Shea said. "I just want to see you dead."

Rondivallo leapt at her.

"Take it easy," said Lance-Corporal Pollitt from behind Palfrey. He pushed through and covered all four of the people here.

The men sprang round.

Rondivallo's little mouth dropped open, and his eyes first opened wide in bewilderment, then narrowed as he backed away.

"Get those hands up," Pollitt said, matter-of-factly.

"And you, miss. Up, I said." He glanced at Palfrey. "All yours now, doc," he finished, and there was a twist of a grin at his lips.

Then the world seemed to go upside down to Matt Stone, for the girl, her arms halfway above her head, looked at Palfrey and said in a voice which was nearly strident:

"Oh, Sap, thank God you've come."

Matt didn't believe his ears.

Maureen O'Shea, calling Palfrey "Sap."

"All right, Maureen," Palfrey said, "go and sit down. Don't worry about her, Pollitt." He moved towards Rondivallo, and it did not seem to matter that the automatic was in his hand, that Rondivallo was looking into his eyes. A short while before Pollitt had looked the most ruthless man alive, but now Palfrey took over. The soldier at the door covered the other two men, the linguists. Pollitt watched the drama of the two main protagonists, Palfrey and Rondivallo: and Matt and the girl watched them as if what happened could change the face of the world.

"If there's a way to stop this slaughter, tell me," Palfrey said. "If there's a way to cure the afflicted, tell me. I don't mean the injection, I mean a quick, safe antidote. If there is, I'll let you stand trial. If there isn't, I'll kill you now."

Rondivallo was gasping for breath, and holding up his hands as if to fend Palfrey off.

"Don't—don't come near me! Don't come near me! There—there isn't anything. If you hurt me, what's happening in England will happen in the rest of the world tomorrow. I mean it! The bacteria are in our

214

foods everywhere, they only need contact with the air to bring them out. I've telephoned my agents in every part of the world. It's *on*, Palfrey. I'm the only one who can call it off. Don't touch me, understand? You'll sign the world's death warrant if you do. Get away from me."

He backed further away.

Maureen O'Shea said very tensely: "Sap, in that cabinet there's a list of all the agents. You could have them stopped at once." When Rondivallo turned towards her almost gibbering, she pointed towards a steel cabinet near the desk, but didn't look away from him. "And there is an antidote and an immunising agent. At least, he says there is. Common salt. Even sea water will do." She was beginning to shiver. "A tablespoonful of common salt, or a pint or two of sea water, taken every four or five hours for a day or two. That makes the blood resistant to the poison."

Rondivallo leapt at her, clenched hands raised, as if he would crush out her life.

"That's enough," Pollitt said, and fired a shot which struck the fat man in the leg. It sent him staggering towards the desk, gasping, sobbing, reaching out for support.

Maureen was standing still.

"Sap," she said chokily, "I couldn't get a message out. No one could get away from here. They couldn't let me go back to the hotel. The only thing I could do was to make Rondivallo think I was in love with him, and pray for a chance to warn you. I—I have helped, haven't I?" She was shivering more violently, and her voice was unsteady, now and again her teeth chattered. "It wasn't a waste of time, was it? It's been so awful, shut in here, living with that beast, knowing what he was doing. He promised me no one would die, and I made myself believe that."

"Take it easy, Maureen," said Palfrey very gently.

215

"No one in this world did a better job." He soothed her momentarily, then turned to the lance-corporal.

"Pollitt."

"Sir."

"Did you say you had a radio mechanic in your party?"

"Yes, sir."

"We want him up here, to start sending messages out."

A door crashed open as he spoke. Not far away, heavy footsteps clattered on the stone floor of the passage. Pollitt swung towards the door. The man with the submachine gun backed from the door to cover the passage and the oncoming men. Maureen O'Shea crumpled up and fell. Matt Stone covered the two linguists. He couldn't think clearly, could only feel: and his feeling was of dread in case this chance of salvation would be snatched away.

Then Pollitt said: "It's okay, sir, it's more of the boys." He drew himself up to attention. "Captain Ord, sir. Lance-Corporal Pollitt speaking. Mission completed."

An officer whom Palfrey had not seen before came briskly into the room.

"Good work, corporal. Hallo, sir." He saluted, took the situation in at a glance, and looked back at Palfrey, grinning. "We rounded up fifty-odd of the men who hadn't been infected and got them into safety kit. They've taken over completely downstairs. Found big stores of automatic weapons in the cellar, too, and other arms are believed to be in one of the plants, but the situation here is under control. Anything we can do, sir?"

Matt Stone found himself laughing. It was ridiculous, but he was laughing. No one seemed to think it extraordinary. Palfrey was grinning. Pollitt was, too. Rondivallo was muttering gibberish to himself.

"Yes," Palfrey said, and he was smiling, although sweat

was running down his forehead. "I want radio communication established with 10, Downing Street as soon as possible, and then radio telephone communication established with New York, Sydney, Paris . . ."

Within an hour, all Z5 agents throughout the world were reporting to the national authorities where they worked. Within the same hour, messages were going out to all nations from the Cabinet Room. Rondivallo's agents were rounded up in raids on all World Wide plants. Within that hour, Domminy died from self-administered potassium cyanide, but Rondivallo was still alive. It seemed as if the shock had turned him into a maniac, all he did was to mutter and gibber.

Within an hour, everyone in the country who was suffering, or might suffer, from the bite of the mosquito had been given a solution of common salt, or sea water.

By morning, tens of thousands were still ill, but few more had died and many had completely recovered.

"Well, we can go down on our knees and be thankful that didn't come off," Palfrey said on the following day. He was at the hotel in the forest, where Z5 men and women were in complete possession. He was in the big room overlooking the forest, even that part which had been despoiled by the fire and which looked like a huge black ring against the pale, sunlight green of the rest of the trees. A few white clouds floated across the sky. It was warm in this room, and warmer outside.

Matt was sitting on a couch, with Kathleen O'Shea on one side, Maureen on the other. That had been accident, not design. Stefan Andromovitch sat in the largest chair that the hotel could boast, and looked much too large for it. Several other Z5 members were there, and two blackcoated, precise-looking men, who had come here at the Prime Minister's request: the Minister for Health and the Minister for War.

"There isn't a lot we don't know," Palfrey went on, almost as if he was talking to himself. "Rondivallo discovered the bacteria when experimenting with the radioactive dust in the air. He saw how they could paralyse and silence, and often kill. No one realized that Rondivallo was a megalomaniac who had seen the possibilities if a single man, with a small group of devoted supporters, could control the only weapons of both attack and defence. According to some of the prisoners we've taken, he had been experimenting for years with a drug which could paralyse people temporarily, rendering them quite useless, and he found several—curare, of course, is the drug which atrophies the muscles but leaves the nervous system unaffected. He experimented widely when it was discovered that some animal life was paralysed for a long time after being infected by this particular bacteria, which bed in an insect which looked like a mosquito. The bacteria left the carrier insect but hovered near until dispersed by wind.

"He had been working with Domminy for some time. Domminy was a fanatic on the need for destroying arms, believing that if there were no arms there could be no wars." Palfrey drew his hand across his forehead, then began to wind a few strands of hair round his forefinger. "Who can really say he was wrong?"

"Domminy didn't know that Rondivallo was after world domination, or that at each of the Wide World plants there was a small troop of highly trained ex-soldiers, stores and weapons, everything they would need to create a world secret police. The plague-infested insects were easy to breed, and did not mature until they were exposed to the warmth of daylight; they matured quickest in sunlight. So they were easy to store in warehouses, shops, hotels, army establishments, private

218

homes—everywhere. We know that Rondivallo meant to spread them throughout England, and already had them in many places, including the military establishments. In the largest of these establishments one or two of his men were planted, to release the mosquitoes whenever required.

"I needn't labour that point," Palfrey went on, and stopped fiddling with his hair. "Perhaps a few explanations about the Department's part in this are called for. We were worried about Rondivallo for some time, and when he came to England, Maureen O'Shea"—he looked across at her, and smiled—"agreed to work on him. She had to appear hopelessly infatuated, and became his mistress. Up to the time that she disappeared, she had reported that he was experimenting secretly, but she did not then know that he was concerned with Wide World Foods. Whether Rondivallo suspected her, or whether he simply made sure that no one who knew anything about the plot itself could contact the outside world, we'll never know. But when he thought it time, he disappeared, taking her with him. They lived in the underground quarters at the Lauriston plant, there was a cinema, ordinary home amusements, most things she could want; and there were several families, so that there was communal life. But everyone who knew about the existence of the insects and the bacteria was completely divorced from the outside world.

"So Maureen could not get a word through, and her sister went to look for her, knowing nothing of the truth. There was another woman, Yvonne Brown"—Palfrey looked at Matt—"who was the grand-daughter of the Arbuthnot Brown who originally owned the house which became the Forest Hotel. She often came here on a visit, and because of her association no one suspected that she worked for us.

"Her brother, the last male of the line, was killed on another of our jobs," Palfrey went on, "and it affected

Yvonne deeply. She became aloof, unfriendly, unsociable. But we needed her help because of her knowledge of the district. That's why we sent her to you, Matt.

"Because then we believed that the secret was in the Forest.

"Rondivallo spent a lot of time in a small cottage on the experimental farm, so that it looked as if he was continuing with his ordinary researches, but it was a phony setup. When we took over the hotel he set fire to that section of the forest, hoping we wouldn't look beyond it. Actually he had always done his main work in the underground laboratories at the food plant.

"He had virtually bought not only the hotel but the hotel staff. Larsen and his wife ran the hotel for them. Larsen was another Domminy, a fanatical pacifist; when he realized Rondivallo's real purpose he tried to telephone Domminy, but Domminy was out. And one of Rondivallo's men poisoned Larsen and his wife before he could try again.

"Some of the research chemists and managers at the plant lived at the hotel, which was a reporting point. None of Rondivallo's overseas agents ever went straight to the plant. All reports were made to the hotel and then taken from there to the plant headquarters by delivery vans driven by trusted agents. The organization was as nearly fool-proof as they could make it."

Palfrey paused for a moment, but soon went on:

"We now know that some of the affected food was taken out of the plant in error. These included deliveries made to some Conne village shops. The first to hatch out were those at Mrs Hill's. Doctors Korven and Dimmock each examined Mrs Hill during the period when the infection of the larynx showed clearly. It was examination of this, and experiments with sputum and swabs taken from the throat, which first put doctors on to the curare distillation, and would have put them on to common salt, which builds up a resistance in the blood. So Rondivallo had to cover up quickly.

"Once the two doctors were murdered we knew we were likely to concentrate on the Conne area. We did so. He knew some of our agents, who had been tracing his movements in several parts of the world, and infected them so that it would not appear to be an isolated case, at Conne. Maureen O'Shea says that he first did this in the hope of preventing us from concentrating on Conne. He didn't want us to connect the trouble with Wide World Foods, and was prepared to do anything to distract us. But once he unleashed the plague it had to be done swiftly—he'd have little time to play with. Killing the two doctors was a must, as they would have put us on the right lines to find an immunizing agent; and drawing our attention from Conne was also a must.

"But events moved too fast for him.

"The Carters sold a lot of produce to Wide World, and Carter himself had once worked for Smith, who had killed a man once before. Carter suspected Smith of the murders and accused him. Smith pacified him, but quickly had him killed—as Matt Stone saw.

"Larry's Hill's death, as well as Yvonne Brown's seizure, were not planned. The plague simply got out of control in the district. As we've since seen, only about one victim in two dies. Yvonne Brown is one of the lucky ones, and is now responding to treatment.

"One of the disturbing factors from our point of view was the fact that Domminy and Rondivallo knew so many Z5 agents." Palfrey went on. "They seem to have identified them simply by watching everyone looking for Rondivallo. Matt Stone and Yvonne were suspected when they reached the Forest Hotel, and we know how Domminy tried to discredit Stone by giving a false message from Washington to the Prime Minister.

"There's very little more," Palfrey finished. "There will be a great deal of tidying up after the dislocation in social and economic life, but a week or ten days should see it through. All the breeding grounds for the plague have been found and destroyed. There is no danger left."

"Matt," said Palfrey, a little later, "you probably think that I should have told you about Maureen, and also more about other agents we had in the Conne district. I didn't, because there was a risk you would be caught and made to talk." He smiled faintly. "It wasn't unil later that you seemed a serious security risk!"

Matt said: "Forget it, I'll always remember the speed with which you worked. Tell me one thing more."

"Name it."

"Did you know Kathleen O'Shea was at the hotel?"

"Oh yes. But she seemed exactly what she claimed to be. She's on her way home now."

"That's fine," Matt said. "That's fine."

A few evenings later, when it was nearly dark, he took his gleaming car from the parking space at the hotel and drove towards Oak Tree Hill, where he had gone with Yvonne Brown on that first strange journey. He could picture her profile as clearly as if she was by his side now. The evenings light did not hide the view but gave it a touch of mystery; at least it held no dangers, no hidden causes for dread and for horror.

He heard another car coming up the hill and turned to look at it. Suddenly he realized that Yvonne Brown was at the wheel of an English Ford. She turned off the road and stopped. Matt opened the door for her and saw her long, lovely legs, and remembered the way she had tried to get out of the Chrysler when they had stopped outside the plant. Then the mark of the plague had been on her forehead. Now a tiny scab was hardly noticeable.

"Hallo, there," Matt greeted. "So the place drew you back, too?"

222

"I couldn't keep away," Yvonne said.

"Nor me. It's good to see you well again."

She was silent for a long time. He wondered what was going on in her mind, and remembered that he had never really seen her smile. Was she still obsessed by memory of her brother? Or would she feel now that she had squared his account.

She turned to look at him.

"It's good to see you," she said, and smiled.